INCOMPARABLE
WORLD

INCOMPARABLE
WORLD

a novel by
S. I. MARTIN

GEORGE BRAZILLER PUBLISHER
New York

First published in the United States in 1998 by George Braziller, Inc.

Originally published in Great Britain in 1996 by Quartet Books

Copyright © 1996 by S. I. Martin

For information, please address the publisher:
George Braziller, Inc.
171 Madison Avenue
New York, NY 10016

Library of Congress Cataloging in Publication Data:
Martin, S. I.
    Incomparable world : a novel / by S. I. Martin.
        p.   cm.
    ISBN 0-8076-1436-X
    1. Blacks–England–London–History–18th century–Fiction.
2. Afro-American loyalists–England–London–Fiction. I. Title.
PR6063.A7314I163 1998
823'.914–dc21   98-19986
                                CIP

Printed and bound in the United States

Designed by Rita Lascaro

First edition

I am only a lodger—and hardly that.
—Ignatius Sancho

London, 29 May 1786

Buckram stood in a puddle outside the Charioteer and listened to the shouts and laughter of several black people in the big, smoky room. The alehouse was full this evening, and through a grimy, rain-streaked window he watched his old begging mentor, Georgie George (as wigless as ever), standing in front of the fire, opening and closing his shabby frock coat every few seconds.

There was Henry Prince, the boxer, looking fatter and dressing much better, looking prosperous in fact. Two men (one black, one white) dressed as women were leaning against the bar, screaming for drinks. The publican, Offaly Michael, was still there, bullying his staff and trying to keep order.

He caught a glimpse of Angola Molly—a lifelong whore and at twenty-eight a grandmother. Business as usual, Buckram thought. He scanned the crowd more closely. William wasn't in tonight and Neville, of course, wouldn't be seen dead in such a place.

He caught his own reflection in the green-tinged pane and backed away. He looked over his shoulder at the cramped tenements of Brydges Street. They looked seedy and sagged like poorly baked loaves left in a cold, grimy oven. Even from the street he could smell the sour stench that told of generations of uncleanliness, whores going from one tavern to another, gangs of cadgers huddling at the mouths of alleys and courtyards. Groups of strangers gathered under awnings and talked about the weather. The sky rumbled fitfully and Buckram felt abandoned, at the mercy of an English god.

He thought back to the night before when, too ashamed and confused to return to his old haunts, he'd taken himself to Warren Street, to the Black Sickhouse, for a meal. His bubbling bowels kept him awake throughout the night, while all around him howling madmen expired on verminous mattresses. It was almost as bad as jail, so he escaped before morning and the arrival of the press-gangs.

Three black Grenadier Guardsmen approached the tavern. "Hey, brother!" A tall guardsman was loosening his purse. "Take this!" A handful of pennies landed at Buckram's feet. He scooped up the coins. Having no pockets, he held them in his fist. He looked in again at the irrepressible high spirits behind the window. It was too soon; he couldn't face them in there yet. First of all he needed cheap food and some real friends.

The cookhouse was a long wooden shed with a chain-strung counter giving onto the corner of Cross Lane and Castle Street. Trays of baked potatoes swimming in lard were displayed alongside suet pudding with lumps of fat as large as walnuts. Pea soup, hot eels, and sheep's trotters were arranged on a hot plate to one side. Buckram ordered some soup and a slice of pudding. He handed over two of his three pennies before his food was slopped onto a grimy tin plate chained to the counter. It was the best meal he'd tasted in a very long time. The elflocked Portuguese counterman laughed appreciatively at him. "Straight from the Bridewell, my friend?"

Buckram nodded and felt himself smile through a mouthful of peas and pudding.

He headed down King Street and across Broad Street toward the heart of his old community: St. Giles. Sighing with relief and dread he entered the old rookery at Dyott Street.

It was as if the houses here had originally been one block of stone, now eaten away by giant weevils into numberless small chambers and connecting passages. Home to London's outcasts, this dank, unlit warren attracted a constantly changing population of escaped convicts, runaway slaves, abandoned women, and men without trades. Here the homeless could sleep unmolested, their slumber interrupted only by the waves of shrieks and course chatter from the close-packed, crumbling buildings that encircled them, the walls the color of bleached soot. Thieves and beggars, black and white, splashed across wet alleys, going in and out of each other's homes without ceremony.

Buckram walked around piles of rubbish and small fires in the middle of the street. He was aware that he was being observed, but that was to be expected in the rookery. Everyone watched everyone else. There was no privacy and anything worth hiding soon became public knowledge or public property. Not for the first time did he find reassurance in this naked fact of rookery life. His ragged clothes betrayed no jingle of money or arms, he was a threat to no one, and his dark skin drew no second glances.

He followed the chants of an African melody coming from the alley called Ivy Street where he used to live. The drumbeats and singing from inside the house were amplified in the small courtyard, which sloped to where a pool of sewage lay soaking. Buckram leaped over it and entered the unlocked door.

He walked casually from room to room past doors long fallen from worm-eaten posts. His eyes, accustomed to jail light, discerned figures shuffling about where the darkness turned from gray to black. The musicians were in a top-floor garret, where they intoned incomprehensible chants to a mournful rhythm and stared blankly at a candle on the floor in the middle of the room. Without breaking the music they turned as one to look at him, then refocused on the candle.

He came eventually to the third-floor room that he'd once shared with William and Neville. It was full of strangers—he counted eleven of them, all black men from Africa, America, and the Caribbean. He didn't recognize anybody and no one seemed to notice him, so he felt his way down the staircase and stepped back out onto Ivy Street.

He conducted a halfhearted search of the local inns: the Hampshire Hog and the Little Dublin. They were mostly full of Irish porters and market people, a few black faces, again no one he knew. On a whim, he decided to look in at the Beggar in the Bush. It was somewhere he'd not normally visit; the place was always too lively in the wrong way. When he poked his head around the door a flagonful of ale—he smelled it later on his clothes—was hurled at him. He ran.

In Phoenix Street he paused to watch a calf being slaughtered by the roadside. An immense wave of anxiety rocked him as he turned away from St. Giles and headed toward the brighter lights of town. He caressed his smooth penny and looked at his muddy toes sticking out of a butchered pair of shoes. After years of confinement, he was too scared to sleep in the open and too scared to stop walking. A friendless future yawned before him.

There was nothing else to do; he'd have to return to Covent Garden and face Georgie George.

A tense silence descended on the crowd in the Charioteer as Buckram moved through it. Well-dressed drinkers surrounded him. Rivulets of sweat trickled down his back exciting his more recent sores and welts. Faces skewed with disgust, then with puzzlement and pity. After having been so long in the company of arrogant whites, Buckram had lost the memory of being in a room full of their black counterparts.

There was a weight here, an assumed intimacy that enveloped as it separated. Accurate judgments assailed him and he was being sentenced: ex-slave from the Americas, ex-soldier dumped in London, ex-convict, homeless, childless, my brother, bad penny come round again.

Georgie was seated at a small table, talking close, fast, and low with the three guardsmen who'd helped Buckram earlier that night. On seeing his old student Georgie halted the conversation with a curt gesture. He motioned the men away and composed himself nervously as Buckram approached.

"Well, Georgie? What news?"

Georgie reached out slowly. His normally cheerful, cynical face dropped as he took hold of the callused hand before him.

"Buckram?" He touched the tired man's shirt. It felt like iron, so stiffened was it with dried blood. He touched the wild gray hair, then he looked into those steady, demented eyes and knew for sure. "The Bridewell?"

A pint of Bene Carlo wine appeared in his hands.

"We thought you were dead. Some said you were fitted out for sea." Georgie looked him up and down. "What happened to you?"

The ex-convict, with a stare as vicious and impartial as bird shot, said, "Don't you know?"

For all of one second Georgie George smiled his weakest smile, with hatred. Then suddenly turning aside and raising his drink, the Beggar King cried, "To our old friend, Buckram, back from Bridewell's depths. Three cheers, hip, hip!"

Buckram drank long and deep of his wine, finishing the measure in one unbroken swallow. He smacked his lips. "I needed that. Feels good, so good to be free again."

"Free?" said Georgie. "Free? We're all in prison here, Buckie. You're just out of jail." Georgie raised his beaker. "Don't forget—you're still in the exercise yard. Welcome home, boy. Welcome home."

Against his better judgment, Buckram accepted the sentiments. He desperately wanted to relax, was trying his best to, but the only comforts he could glean from his situation were the facts that he was as safe as he ever could be from physical injury and that he was once more in the company of a black person who spoke his kind language. Shame that person was Georgie George though.

Georgie was beckoning someone to join them. Henry Prince, trying to hide his irritation at having been summoned over with so little subtlety, glided over and slapped Buckram on the back, making him wince. The near giant carried a velvet folder under his arm.

"Well, hello again, soldier. What brings you back to the Charioteer?" he groaned.

"Buckie's been away on His Majesty's Service. But he's back to his old ground now. Back to stay." Buckram sat motionless, staring into his empty jar, daring himself to outdream yet another living nightmare.

"It's funny," Georgie continued. "We were talking about you not so long ago, me and Henry."

The once-famous boxer just scratched his head and looked away across the room.

"Henry's become a man about town, he's famous now. His moneymaking's moved from his knuckles to his fingertips. Our Henry is an author. Toast of London. In great demand. Having some funny distribution problems though over the Court End. Ain't that right, Hen?"

Henry Prince, Buckram now saw, was exhausted from some private sadness. Forcing himself to smile, Henry replied, "Whatever you say, George. Whatever you say."

"Hmmm. Anyway it's good to see a black man get his bread through industry. And a brother like Henry, you know." Georgie jerked his stool around to address Buckram and speak away from the subject. "He's the kind of man who'd rather need somebody to help, if you follow. Give him two friends and he'll make his own crowd. He's always had a lot to give. He just lacks the right people to give to. True or not, Mr. Prince?"

From behind the Beggar King's back Henry produced a sarcastic grunt of assent.

"Hear him?" Georgie nodded swiftly to where Henry sat. "All that work's getting to him."

Buckram grabbed Georgie's sleeve and tugged him closer, out of Henry's earshot.

"George," he asked, "what's really going on here?"

"Our friend here has had family worries. Lost his wife, y'know. You remember her, don't you?"

Buckram summoned up a vague image of Deirdre: serious, frantic, and blonde. Afraid to walk the streets with her husband, she spent her time pacing their room in Drury Lane.

"Left this life by her own fair hand," Georgie added. "Took the child with her. Vitriol." He went on. "Henry here needs a rest, so that's why I mentioned that a sharp mover, an old street hand, someone like you, say, could help him out with the selling, y'know? Easy work. Clean money."

Henry Prince looked at Georgie.

"Hen." Georgie tapped him on the cuff. "Show him what you do."

Henry opened the folder and produced a slim package wrapped in brown paper. He broke the seal and handed Buckram a thin, gray pamphlet. Georgie spelled out the florid lettering on the cover for him: *Aethiopian Secret Papers.*

Buckram turned the page and saw a drawing of a white man enjoying sexual congress with a black woman who looked suspiciously like Angola Molly. He flicked through ten more pages, featuring the same model with different men, combinations of men and inanimate objects. Buckram nodded at a picture of her wielding a bamboo cane over an old white man.

Georgie explained the tiny print in the last five pages: "These are the girls, see? Their names and addresses here, their skills and their fees."

"So what's the problem, Georgie?" asked Buckram. "Don't tell me you can't sell enough of these?"

"Well, in the past we've managed...but now you've got all kinds coming over here, setting up in business: Libyan women, Moluccan women, Lascars, and Chinese to say nothing of the French and Swedes. It's not so easy.

"And on top of that there's the problem of the law, Buckie. It's not like the old days when a black man could just slip a Charlie a pound or two and they'd leave you alone. No, nowadays, they'll take you down Bow Street for a drubbing after they've robbed you. You can help us."

"No!" Buckram flung the papers to the table and rose up before Georgie. "I've had enough of your lies and schemes. All I want from you is what's owing me. What you owe me for two years in that...that..."

Georgie raised his eyebrows in the direction of Henry. The boxer-turned-illustrator took Buckram by the shoulders and settled him back in his chair.

"I just want what's mine, Georgie, with interest. I'm a master horseman, a trained ostler. If you hadn't asked me to join you in..."

"Asked? Buckie, I didn't ask you to join me. That, like this," he said as he pointed at the papers in the folder, "was an invitation. And in any case, d'you think there's a white man out there who'll take on a black horseman? What can I say? I'm always here if you need to discuss any money matters."

Georgie folded his arms and shot a glance at the company. Henry Prince eased a charcoal stick from his waistcoat and started to sketch the Beggar King in his new position.

A dry cackling erupted from the bar. Buckram saw Old Morris, another soldier from the American War, staggering from drinker to drinker. He was crossing himself and pointing at Buckram and Georgie. He reeled to their table, drew up his shoulders and gave a wobbly salute.

"All present and correct, I see." He grinned.

"Greetings, Morris," said Buckram. "Long time."

"I see prison taught you nothing about friendship, Buckie." Morris glared at George. "He's got you again, eh?" He drew a fat forefinger across one of his chins and made a croaking sound.

"Look to yourself, Buckram. Look to yourself, matey." Old Morris crossed himself one more time, then his eyes glazed over and he toppled backward onto the floor.

"Don't mind him," said Georgie, struggling to suppress his contempt. "God knows what drags him here night after night. We all hate him. He's just a slave."

"He's still one of us." Closer to a question than a statement.

"Look at us!" Georgie flung a hand toward the crowd. "Most of us were slaves at one time or another. But him..." He snorted. "He's a slave of his own making."

Lost for words, Buckram conceded the point. That well-fed drunkard had once been one of them. Like Buckram, Henry, William, and Neville, like hundreds of others. Old Morris had been born and raised in America as some white man's property. At the outbreak of war he, like they, had escaped bondage to enlist in the British army and take up arms against his masters. Morris had been a war hero—a spy behind enemy lines and a first-class man-at-arms. But the British lost and whole platoons of black loyalists fled with them. They had all been promised their freedom as a condition of service and they had been promised pensions. But as they boarded the troopships that would take them to London none of the black fighters could have imagined the freedom to which they would be doomed.

In no time at all, the streets of London were flooded with an army of fresh black beggars. Instead of begging down the Court End or along the Strand, Morris chose to rattle his cup in Lincoln's Inn Fields at the door of the Committee for the Settlement of American Claims. He had done this for eight months and, as a result, he became the only American black Buckram knew of who'd received any part of his pension. Money, however, was not the cure for Morris's ailment. He couldn't rest until he had found work in his profession as a gunsmith. For decades blacks had been barred from both apprenticeships and any paid work in a London guild. Morris, though, had managed to keep in contact with his old commanding officer and, on his commendation, finally secured a position in the cannon-boring shed of Grice and Co. In time it transpired that not only was he an unpaid worker but he had sold himself to the proprietor in exchange for a roof over his head, three meals a day, and the opportunity to design newer, deadlier firearms.

Buckram decided that he wasn't in a position to judge. At least Old Morris didn't have to fear for his life. The same couldn't be said of Quintus Greene, now wheeling himself across the floor on a trolley propelled by wooden blocks, and it couldn't be said of Georgie or of Buckram himself. He paused a while to reflect on how much he could get for himself on the open market.

Georgie nudged him. "Ah, look," he said. "Here comes your dinner. It's on the house."

A barmaid slid a plate of boiled mutton and barley across his table. The food was hot and tasty.

"Where's William tonight?"

"We don't see so much of him these days. Not in Brydges Street. Most nights he'll be at that alehouse in Rose Street. He has a place in one of the upstairs rooms there. But he's still the same old William; throwing his money around, trying to dice his way to a fortune."

"And Neville?"

Georgie spat on the floor. "Pastor Neville! He's still around. Sweeps out the churchyard at St. Giles. Best place for him. Lives in his own little world. So, tell me, when did you get out?"

"Yesterday afternoon. Stayed at the Sickhouse last night. Never again."

"Too true. If you get better in there, they'll sell you off to some sea captain bound for America. You'll end up back in chains. You still have your army papers on you?"

"Somewhere. With Neville, I hope."

"Good, well get yourself off to Lisson Grove tomorrow morning. If you don't want to work with us, they're giving out money to black beggars at the sign of the Yorkshire Stingo."

Buckram tried to imagine what a Yorkshire Stingo looked like.

"Sixpence, every day. But get there early, before the rush. Or, if you're fast you can call over at the White Raven, Mile End in the morning; they're doing the same thing there too, then you can make it to the Stingo by the afternoon."

"Sixpence, eh?" Buckram stroked his chin, wary as he always was when he could see no reason for white men's generosity.

A Jamaican barber, whose name Buckram had forgotten, brought over another measure of wine and a clay pipe packed with hemp leaves. Buckram tipped a burning candle to the bowl and sucked hard. He blew a column of smoke fumes over the dark beams in the ceiling. He puffed slowly, letting the smoke fill his lungs. Georgie snatched the pipe from him and said, "You're not ready for this yet. Give it some time. A few days. Drink now."

Suddenly there was a firm hand on his forearm preventing him from lifting the wine. After two years in jail Buckram knew better than to turn too quickly. He glanced at Georgie who was scowling up at the newcomer.

"Wine is a mocker," said the stranger. "Strong drink is raging, and whosoever is deceived thereby is not wise."

"Pastor Neville!" shouted Buckram and jumped up to embrace his old comrade-in-arms from Carolina.

"How did you know where to find me? I've just come from Ivy Street. Who told you I was out?"

"Out?" He looked at his mate. "So it's true, then. It was the House of Correction. Cold Bath Fields?" Neville shivered, savoring that name for jail.

"No, Bridewell," Buckram corrected him.

Neville made a sound between a grunt and a groan. "I followed you from Broad Street. I thought it was you, but I couldn't believe what my eyes were telling me. So I had to enter this...this...sink of iniquity, in my quest for the truth."

Of all the old campaigners now living in London, Neville Franklin was the only one who had retained his dignity. But he was mad. He still wore his Royal Ethiopian Regiment uniform with the motto "Liberty to Slaves" stitched across the shoulders. He still quoted the Bible.

He was a tall gloomy man in his late thirties. When not speaking the Bible, Neville muttered in tongues and focused on infinity. He glowered at the debauchees in the tavern one by one.

The two men in women's clothing pulled scented hand-kerchiefs from their bosoms and waved them at him.

"Buckram," he muttered, his voice growing to a bellow, "what place is this! Behold these sons of Sodom, flaunting themselves in Satan's raiments." Neville turned to address the crowd while pointing at the transvestites. "I have espied such as these taking the walk from Clare Market to the Piazza, seeking to entice youth unto like corruption. Verily, the Lord shall smite thee in thy gin-soaked citadels as he did smite the Cities of the Plain. Thrice accursed art thou, Seed of Bab..."

"Oi," hollered Offaly Michael from the other side of the room. "None of your sermons in here. Either drink or get out. He with you, George?"

Reluctantly, Georgie spread his arms to include Buckram and Henry. "He's with us."

"Neville," Buckram implored. "Please be seated."

The Christian remained standing.

"Oooh! This is what I call a real welcome home, Buckie

boy," sneered Georgie. "Us old soldiers have to stick together."

"You, an old soldier?" Pastor Neville sucked his teeth. "Don't play that line with me, Georgie George. We all know how you came to be here."

"What are you saying, exactly, preacher? Are you calling me a liar?"

Unable to make up with abuse what he lacked in wit, Neville took refuge in scripture. "The guilty fleeth where none pursueth. Indeed, I am calling you a liar. You have borne false witness. And more."

A service bayonet appeared in Georgie's right hand. It bobbed in front of Neville's face. The crowd parted, giving Georgie more room in which to commit murder.

In a calm, loud voice Neville said, "You will put down that weapon, Mr. George. Violence covereth the mouth of the wicked. My friend Buckram and I will now hold counsel together. Alone."

Slowly, Georgie let the bayonet's heavy point rest on Neville's cheek, just beneath his eye.

"Fool," he said, and slid the blade harmlessly down the preacher's stubble. He passed the unfinished pipe back to Buckram and withdrew with Henry to the bar.

"Of all places," said Neville as he took Georgie's seat, "you had to come here. To sit with him after what he did to you."

"Neville, Georgie is...Georgie. What he did was a mistake. As a Christian you should find it in yourself to forgive him." Buckram re-lit the pipe.

"No, never. Georgie George doesn't make mistakes."

Neville was right, of course. Georgie never made mistakes. And everyone did know how he came to be in London.

Three years before they'd been stuck in the port of New York, looking for a way out of the American States. His Majesty's Government had promised safe passage to Jamaica, Nova Scotia, or Britain to any black man who could prove he'd served with the loyalist forces and it soon became apparent that not everyone who wanted to leave would be able to do so. New York, the last British stronghold, was teeming with thousands of black militiamen, all searching for their old commanding officers, or any British official, to vouch for their service records.

And every Wednesday at Fraunces' Tavern, from ten in the morning till two in the afternoon they would assemble to have their "General Birch Certificates" examined by stony-faced army clerks. The rumor was that the man now known as Georgie George, a footman in the service of a wealthy Virginia planter, had escaped with a sackful of his master's plate and jewels and quite a sum of money.

By the time he arrived in New York delegations of masters were also gathering in the town to petition General Carleton, the commander-in-chief, for the return of their slaves. In no time slave catchers were abroad on the streets of the city. Old black campaigners were seized in the streets or dragged from their beds.

According to the story, the original Georgie George was an army storekeeper in the Black Pioneers who was murdered by the Virginia runaway, who took his name and his certificate.

At the time, Buckram and Neville were hiding with

William Supple and his family in a shop cellar near Bowling Green. William had trekked from Carolina with his wife Mary and their children to seek passage on a ship, any ship, leaving for British territory. Like Buckram's and Neville's, William's papers were in order; the three men spent their time trying to figure how best to save his family from a return to bondage. But nothing could be done to save them. Every ship leaving the harbor was full. There were only places for officials, certified soldiers, and horses. William insisted that he'd get them to London somehow, but Mary had begun to despair. She spoke of cutting their losses and fleeing to the free black towns of Nova Scotia before it was too late.

Buckram's last memory of America was the sight of William Supple, Mary, and their two boys waving him and Neville goodbye from the quayside. He was not to meet up with William again for another year.

"You'll stay with me tonight," commanded Neville.

"Thank you, Neville. You've saved my life. Another night in the Sickhouse would have been my last."

Outside the wind was picking up, causing chaos in the street. Slates and gutters were dislodged and everyone gathered at the window to watch the signboard at the Denmark Coffeehouse swing from side to side, higher and higher. They cheered when it fell.

Some of the more adventurous theatergoers were now leaving Drury Lane and hurrying into Brydges Street for drinks.

"Well, Buckram. It really is good to have you back with

us." It was Georgie; somehow he'd materialized behind him as they stood looking out of the window.

"We're off next door to the Three Hairs; buck up on some old buds."

"Whites?"

Georgie shrugged. "And what? A bud's a bud. Anyway, you know them. It's Roughjack and Pete Fortune. They still ask after you. Truth to tell, it's crowbar bouncing we're a-planning."

"Where, when, what's the count?"

Buckram couldn't believe he'd just asked that. So strong was the habit, it had slipped from him unchecked.

"It's for Tuesday night. I hear the Earl of Dartmouth leaves London by the Dover Road. With his town house empty and him out through Fortune's part of Kent, could be double gain to play the prospect both ends. You're welcome to join us." He glanced at Neville. "Though I don't suppose you will. Hmmm, remember my offer anyway, *Aethiopian Secret Papers,* your route to success." He went once more around the tavern, chatting and joking, before returning to Buckram's side. Pulling him away from Neville he spoke into his ear: "Tell me, what would you do if you had two thousand pounds? Where would you go with that sort of money? As a black man, I mean."

Buckram didn't have to think long. "Africa," he said. "I'd be there tomorrow had I the money today. Why?"

"That's an interesting answer, Buckie. I was just wondering if you had one. That's all. A good night to you now."

Georgie left the Charioteer accompanied by Henry and the barmaid.

A gust of wind blew the front door open. Nobody

moved. Neville stepped into the gale and Buckram felt everybody's eyes upon him. He looked over to see Neville signaling, like a farmer calling his hound.

William was carried a short way through the riot before being dropped in mud. Someone approached him with a horse, another with a length of rope. This was starting to look like New York at the evacuation. He found himself garbling a frantic prayer for his wife, Mary, and his sons, Nehemiah and Phillip. The family he'd left on the other side of the world.

"Grab his feet," someone said.

"Get the neck," said another.

Cold, heavy rain fell on his body while the hooligans debated whether to horse-haul or hang him. Rag-shod feet kicked around his head. The arguments over his fate grew fiercer, poignards were drawn, and voices raised.

William flopped over. The puncture in his side sang out in agony with each beat of his heart. He rolled to a crouch and crawled to a hobble, then he was up, clutching his side, shambling through the rabble.

His body knew where he was going. He skidded down the street and staggered against swarms of looters. He felt that he stood out too much, dressed as he was and heading in the wrong direction, so he wedged himself into a doorway and shed his coat and, with reluctance, his waistcoat. He ripped off his wig and smeared his shoes and stockings with mud. His shirt was torn and bloodied enough to pass inspection.

As he studied the mob, he noticed a trickle of people moving away from the destruction. It dawned on him that they were shuffling toward Haymarket with children in tow; they were families in flight. Most of them were still dressed in their St. James finery but others, like him, had attempted to dress down and were artlessly mangling their vowels in an effort to blend in with the crowd. The exit to Haymarket was jamming up with incomers. William was trapped. He'd have to move fast.

He stepped back into the turmoil and took his chance. He flapped his arms and caught the attention of the leader of the next rush of roughs to bubble through the press.

"Ahoy, Blackbird!" said the big, blue-chinned man with tiny green eyes. He wore the blackened clothes of a coal-hauler. "What news, matey? Where's the rumbling?"

"Over there!" William pointed out a party of escapers slinking by the wall of a gutted mansion. "Quality folk, courtenders, shoals of 'em. Have at 'em, lads!"

The "people of quality" were pounced on before they had time to soil their linen.

"And there's some more. Look!" William drew their attention to a band of cowering burghers dressed in their night clothes. The men carried backswords but they weren't given the chance to use them. The mob fired pistols at point-blank range.

Above the confusion, William heard a child scream. It was a scream he'd heard before. This time it was clear and unmistakable: "Turn it aaaaaaaaht! Turn it aaaaaaaaht!"

The boy was sitting on the shoulders of the brute who'd proposed William's hanging. The man-boy monster came lurching toward him as the remaining members of the original crew fell in behind.

Thugs were still bursting into the street and William

heard his pursuers growling behind him as they cuffed their way through the new arrivals. But his ruse was working. The crush was thinning out as the invading hooligans joined in the fray surrounding the well-to-do people. Moving sideways and holding his breath, William squeezed his way through the mass of bodies till he reached Haymarket.

Haymarket was blocked with overturned carriages and footloose livestock. Four or five brewer's carts were being unloaded at the top of the thoroughfare. Casks and barrels rolled down to the thirsty rioters below. Jugs of gin passed from hand to hand and the gutters ran red with wine.

Here and there couples still strolled arm in arm, gazing amusedly at the vandals at play, while late-night revelers sang happy songs in praise of the mayhem around them. Behind the sightseers lay the Moroccan Embassy. A black footman worked there with whom William was on nodding terms. But as he neared the building his heart sank. Another gang was already busy at the doors with a battering ram.

A second destination came to mind. Clutching his side, he fled down Haymarket. He spun right onto Pall Mall and raced to the corner of Albany Street. It was almost quiet here. Only the sobs of women being violated in doorways and the trails of smoke from the Almack Rooms on Pall Mall showed that the rioters had been through. With any luck he could make it to Mrs. Sancho's shop in Charles Street. He was not a friend of the Sancho family, but every black Londoner knew of them. They sold palm oil, hair pomade, and dried fish. It was the only black-owned grocery in town; they were known to keep a collection of firearms. They had to help him.

He paused to take stock, checking that there was no one

behind him. He gazed at his wound—it looked like a slice of veal cake. He was bent almost double as he peered around the corner. Groups of rioters had already broken through to Charles Street and were looting their way down the road. He was too tired and frightened to move out of the way.

He watched as their numbers grew. One wave rushed off to attack Piccadilly, another swelled back up to St. James Square. He hobbled along toward Old Paved Alley; one of his English gambling cronies lived there. It was worth a try.

For some reason a Turkish proverb came into his head. "A drowning man will clutch at a snake."

At the bottom of the street William could see guardsmen at St. James Palace fixing bayonets, priming muskets, and closing the gates against the inevitable attack.

Another howl arose as the vandals appeared in Pall Mall, hard on the heels of three men they'd flushed out from St. James Square. They were black men in Grenadier Guards' uniforms, sprinting toward the barracks and toward William. He staggered into their path, flailing his arms. Two of the guardsmen ran into him, grabbed an armpit apiece and dragged him backward through the closing gates of St. James Palace.

William saw the mob gaining on them as they covered the last fifteen yards to the barracks: a bellowing, red-faced army. The four black men collapsed inside the courtyard just as a volley of glassware, half-bricks, table legs and a dead cat came flying over the battlements. One of the rioters, too eager in the chase, had made it into the barracks on their heels. Seven blades ran through him before he had time to regret his folly.

William's saviors drew their sabers and retreated with him and a number of their company to the safety of stone walls. They carried him up crumbling stairs. He noticed the heavy dampness permeating the interior. And was that a battering ram that he heard?

Red-coated black men, soldiers of the king, were placing him on a soft, downy mattress. He exhaled a thankful sigh as nameless thoughts, cozy and tranquil as feathers landing in fresh sawdust, enveloped him.

It wasn't so much a house as a shed.

"This," asked Buckram, "is where you live?"

"The dwelling place of the Most High."

Pastor Neville's home was a windowless wood-slatted structure held together by shipwrights' nails and tar. The hut abutted a stable in St. Giles's churchyard. A smell of hops and malt from Meux's Brewery blanketed the neighborhood.

Buckram sighed as Neville wrestled a key in a rusty lock. They had both slept in worse places.

Neville lit a dim, smoky lamp and weak light bled over a bed of rotting sacks. Cooking utensils and open books lay facedown in the mess. The walls were cold and moisture dripped to a broken flagstone floor. But Buckram's only thought was of the hours of uninterrupted sleep awaiting him.

Neville left the shack, returning moments later with a half bale of fresh straw.

"My bed, I suppose?"

"Aye, sir, fashion it as you please."

Buckram hefted the bale under his arm and started to

shred it, spreading handfuls of hay across his sleeping area. He added another layer, shaking out the clumps this time, in order to keep the whole soft. He padded the remaining straw high around the walls to ward off drafts and to lessen the chance of injury should he thrash about in his sleep. Only when he'd finished did he realize that he'd made a night bed for a horse.

"Stay away from George," said Neville, "and keep out of the Charioteer."

"Those men are my friends, Neville. It was good to be with them tonight."

"They are friends to no one. Least of all to you. They have done this to you. They made you like this." He framed his hands at the sides of Buckram's stiff, dirty clothes.

Buckram nodded glumly. Friends or not, the regulars at the Charioteer were the only people he knew who could make things happen for him.

It was all right for Neville, he could read and write. He had his verger's post to keep him in food and lodging, but Buckram had lived as a beggar. He knew the horror of competing and sometimes fighting with the legions of native poor (crossing themselves whenever you crossed their path), your gaze never leaving the ground for fear of missing the scraps that will feed you for another day. Each day finds you looking more and more bedraggled as, one by one, you give up your dreams. He would never live like that again. He would kill himself first.

"That man is the very devil. He could have saved you in your hour of need. Instead he let you suffer in his place. You endured prison for that rogue and still, not one day free, you seek his company. Verily, as the dog returneth to his vomit, so shall the fool to his folly. A pox on him!"

It was true, Georgie George had betrayed him. And all because of a chicken and a dog.

Buckram positioned himself tenderly on his bed. He listened to the patter of rain on the roof and enviously watched Neville reading in the corner beneath the swaying light until he could watch no more.

In his sleep he dreamed of Africa, an Africa he'd never known. The scene was a forest clearing—everywhere was hot and damp, just like Virginia in August. Smoke rose from chimneys, grass huts had windows, and all the people dressed in the same cloth, the slave material: buckram. Roasting meats turned on spits. The whole village sang, call and response, with the rhythms in the background.

Warm breezes gathered under his outstretched arms and carried him, spiraling slowly, into the sky.

"But you cannot fly, you who have never known Africa," a voice informed him.

"I know that," he replied.

Beneath him, the village shrank, suddenly becoming a blur in a forest on the bank of a river protected by plains from the shadow of the sea.

He was caught in cold wild air above the clouds, hauled up above the curving earth.

"Let me dream. To the devil with ye! Just for once, let me dream!"

But dreaming again, he remembered.

He was running through Carolina nights and breaking into storehouses. American militia men were everywhere and some place ahead was Cornwallis's army, massed and encroaching, with weapons he could use. He lay low till he was met by loyalist scouts.

He was interrogated before being recruited and given a small pistol. A week later he was digging latrines and graves outside a jail pen in a hailstorm. Three other black men worked with him, their red armbands slipping as they chipped through the rock. They worked like that for a whole winter: Buckram, Neville, William, and the fourth, a forgotten man who was found one day, frozen to death in a praying position.

When thousands of white loyalists deserted back to their homesteads for harvest time, the ex-slaves were ordered to fight. And they followed the armies through weeks of hunger and days of plenty, when they enjoyed the meat, ale, cornmeal, and sometimes girls they found abandoned in those vast, empty plantations where they might have slaved.

Then it was summer, bringing more death and more hunger. Graveyard duty under a burning sun. Shallow graves only. And for some corpses just a covering of logs, tree bark, and rocks. It was a season of stomach cramps, for they ate what they could: green ears of August corn boiled with the thinnest strips of lean beef and green peaches. They ate everything except the horses.

Buckram loved the horses. Time spent with them was time away from death and disease. It was the nearest he'd come to free time.

And all the while, throughout the war and throughout the dream, Neville and his Bible readings; doleful psalms and grim monodies promising deliverance.

Suddenly Neville's voice was gone, to be replaced by the

African drumming and lamentations from Ivy Street. He was back in the late campaign, just after they'd taken Camden, Carolina. He was carrying his sword-pistol and William was holding a bayonet. As usual, after a battle, they were moving through a section of outhouses, on a whim, just the two of them, pillaging and looking for stray rebels to kill. And as usual, they found them: unarmed white men whom they'd hack to death simply for the pleasure of ignoring their cries for mercy.

They are all around him now, calling him out of slumber. He sits up sharply. He listens.

The roosters of St. Giles's High Street have curdled his sleep, and the nightmare slips away. He wakes just another man without a woman, his dream already forgotten.

London, 30 May 1786

"Well, how d'you feel now?"

William lay on the mattress, propped up by three of the largest, softest pillows he had ever seen. Like the dressings on his wounds, they were spotlessly clean and scented with lavender. The bandages felt tight and good around his ribs and he felt absolutely no pain whatsoever. They gave him a bowl of wheat boiled in milk and spiced with nutmeg and a copy of the *Public Advertiser.* On the other side of the small, tidy mess a black guardsman was frying sausages and mushrooms. A tabby cat stretched out in a pool of morning sunlight and watched a heavy can of hot China tea being brought in.

These were regular troops but they were not real soldiers, not fighting men. They were buglers, fife-tootlers, drummers, and triangle-ticklers—ornamental warriors and musical mascots. He'd seen black men like this before, pampered regimental pets who paraded in turbans. They wouldn't have lasted an hour in the ranks of the Royal Ethiopians. But they lived well and that was the important thing.

"So, you're a musician then?" The sausage-fryer was holding William's flageolet.

Since last night he'd decided to stop calling himself an actor. He'd been on stage only once, and then as an understudy at Drury Lane Theatre for Behn's *Oroonoko*. His other performance was as King of the Moors in Lord Mayor's pageant two years before. His friends still mocked him for it; he had dressed in a pink and green tunic with an acquamarine sash, a high-plumed turban, baggy Turkish trousers, and bejeweled Turkish slippers. In his right hand he had carried a gold-painted sword that he used to fend off the swatting lion on his left. It was time to stop acting, he decided, time to play himself.

"I'm a gambler," he admitted. "And I live above the Coopers' Arms, the cockpit in Rose Street."

The soldiers gathered round him with new interest. They were all young men, none older than twenty. Smooth-faced and innocent-looking, they chattered in an African tongue and it was some moments before he realized that they were triplets.

They chatted for a while about cockpits, comparing the merits of the Royal in Birdcage Walk against the New Red Lion in Clerkenwell. Of course, they'd never heard of his pit. Black people rarely went there.

He felt himself relaxing, the full sunlight through clean glass pressing him back into the pillows. One of the triplets shook him by the shoulders. "Come, brother. You can't stay here. We have to go to work."

They were now dressed in braided jackets and white waistcoats. Scarlet pantaloons were worn with yellow Hessian boots, tasseled with black silk. And there on their heads sat the inevitable plumed turbans. William smiled to himself and got up to change into his soiled clothes.

"It's Vauxhall again," muttered the tea bearer as he arranged, then re-arranged, his sash. "The Pleasure Gardens. Them Assembly Room types pay for a company of Guards to go down every week to escort them. Safe out, safe back. You ever been there?"

William shook his head.

"Don't go. Crowd down there's unholy. They don't pay us for this," he said as he pointed to his cornet, "they pay us for this." He peeled back the top of his right boot to reveal the hilt of a small dirk.

"How much do they pay you, these types?" asked William.

"The colonel gets twenty-five pounds for our hire, the sergeant fifteen pounds, the musketeers ten, and we get eight pounds, ten shillings."

"Each?"

"Each."

Willlam was dumbstruck. That was a phenomenal amount of money for an honest day's work.

"All this money...what do you do with it? Why do you still live here? I mean where do...how...I mean...WHAT do you do with it?"

They giggled softly and exchanged a few phrases in their own language. "You want to know what we do with our money? Come and find out. The last Friday of every month we have a party. A private affair in Bull Inn Court, Covent Garden. No whites. Only five shillings. And we're playing."

"I'll be there." It was a lot of money for a night out but that had never worried him in the past.

He marched out of the mess behind the guardsmen and true to the custom of this new land, where names had no meaning, he introduced himself only when they parted.

He thanked Newton, Charles, and Hercules.

Outside the barracks the last few looters were still prowling the streets of St. James.

William needed a good, strong drink of porter, but his purse had been stolen. He avoided the built-up areas of the Court End and headed toward St. James Park, where he knew he could find Georgie George.

The Beggar King was sitting on his usual bench by the canal. Behind him the walls of Buckingham House fringed the tops of the lilac trees, and young ladies and their gentlemen sauntered in the first truly fine weather of the year. Georgie waved to nurses and children promenading on the grassy banks. Beside him was a small pewter pail.

"Hail, Willie!"

"Hail, Georgie!"

"What brings you onto the streets at this hour?"

"I've had a wild night, George. A wild night."

Georgie scrutinized his friend's bruised face and mud-spattered clothes.

"Yes, I know what you mean." He nodded, tapping an ivory-topped cane and fingering a gold watch chain, neither of which he'd had the day before.

Georgie inclined his head toward William and whispered, almost conspiratorially, "Buckram's back."

"He's alive?"

"Yes. Walked into the Charioteer last night. He's been in the Bridewell. Didn't have a very good time of it. He asked after your health."

"He spoke to you?!?" William had noticed a strange

smile creeping over Georgie's face as he spoke. This was typical of him. He had been the first to greet Buckram on his release even though he was almost certainly involved in his incarceration. William had heard the rumors, but he was no different from anyone else. In times of trouble people went to Georgie, and in times of plenty Georgie came to you.

"He's staying with friend Neville for the time being. I don't think he's very well." Georgie touched his forehead three times. "Does that to a man, sometimes, jail."

"That takes more than jail, Georgie, and we both know it."

They sat in silence for a moment or two, watching some swans attacking the park wardens who had come to feed them. In the pail at Georgie's side, under a scrap of muslin, dead pigeons and squirrels lay heaped.

"I've got to see Buckram. Where is he now?"

"You'll most likely find him up by Lisson Grove, at the Stingo with all the other sadblacks, signing for their sixpence." Georgie kissed his teeth and spat.

"But we've all begged, my friend. It's nothing to be ashamed of. You are the Beggar King, you should know this."

"William." Georgie looked him straight in the eye for the first time ever. "William, I do not beg. I have never begged. Have you ever seen me cap in hand? Have you ever known me to ask a stranger for money? A landlord for shelter? A woman for her quim?"

William thought about this, and was still thinking about it when a party of well-heeled folk ambled by and wished Georgie a good morning. They tipped their hats and each placed a coin in his pail. As they passed, Georgie shouted something incomprehensible at their backs and they burst into laughter. Turning back to William, his face reset to that mask of cold disdain.

"You'll be needing money if you are going out of town." He produced a pound note. "Here. Pay me back later."

William accepted the money and, like the rest of London town, tipped his hat to Georgie George.

Walking away, he heard the Beggar King shout, "Give my regards to friend Buckie when you see him!"

William gave him a laugh he didn't know he had, a laugh he didn't want to hear again.

Somewhere along Oxford Street, Buckram found himself behind a group of twenty black men. Most were wearing rags, a few were on crutches, and one man was being hauled along on a clumsy A-frame stretcher. They carried quarterstaffs and walked six abreast along the wide pavement. They were obviously on their way to Lisson Grove so he ran and caught up with them. They accepted his company without comment.

They passed fantastic window displays of multi-colored crystal flasks, decorative firearms, and chinaware. Even the fruit and vegetables looked outlandish here: waxed and polished apples and pears, pyramids of pineapples, oranges, figs, and grapes. Startled pedestrians stepped around them, frightened by such a large foreign presence. The only insults came from windows above street level.

Buckram was sure he recognized some of these men from his previous beggary; one of them gestured to him. Buckram shrugged in his general direction. The man was well-built, hearty, and looked as if he were having a good time. His clothes were more battered than tattered and had been of good quality not so long ago. He came across to Buckram.

"You don't remember me?"

Buckram shook his head.

"Julius," the man continued, "Julius Bambara. I know you from Ratcliffe, I'm sure of it. You used to live there in Angel Court, off Blue Gate Fields with that Bible man, the quiet one, Neville. It's Buckram, isn't it? I knew I'd seen you before."

Julius grabbed Buckram's hand and pumped it vigorously, stopping only when he noticed its gruesomely callused wrist.

"You're looking...good," said Julius, registering the changes in his old acquaintance.

Buckram felt his mouth spreading to a thin grin, but his mind was empty. He knew who Julius was now.

On his arrival in this city, three years previously, he and Neville had lived for two drunken months with Julius and his sailor friends in a lodging house down by the docks. It had been winter and they had slept on bare floorboards and damp pallets in unfurnished rooms with ceilings the color of old leather. Julius and his friends all worked on slave ships whenever they got the chance. For them, Ratcliffe was a temporary home to which they returned every six months. Their neighbors were mostly East Indians and black runaways.

Now and then, when one of the sailors had money, a group of them would traipse through the city to Covent Garden, where they'd spend nights with whores at the Cider Cellar on Maiden Lane.

Buckram had always found Julius's company depressing. The merry sailor spoke incessantly about himself and his seafaring exploits. Immune to other people's suffering, he wielded his own joy like a cudgel. It was unsettling to see how little he had altered, how far they both hadn't come. He let the man babble on.

"Now, Buenos Aires, Argentina. Buckie, that's a city for a black man. The girls they have there! You never want to leave. They have these Bangala parties, real African parties with the masks, drums, and everything and everybody just lines up to receive the spirits. I was there eight months, a girl every night and all the quality assemblies. You should go there, one day...find out what life is all about."

Julius went on to show him a lurid ring supposedly won from the owner of the largest emerald mine in Brazil. That was the place. Buckram should get over there some time. As for him, he was sailing out to the Gold Coast in two days' time. Just in London to see some friends.

"What are you doing here? Why are you walking with us?" Buckram realized he'd spoken.

"Weeell, I was at James Street, in the Nag's Head the other night. Dicing. I lost everything except these clothes and this ring. A friend told me to meet him at the Stingo. They're giving money away, he said. So, here I am."

"It's only sixpence."

"It's still money." Julius twisted the ring off his little finger and pocketed it. "I look like a beggar now, don't I?"

They turned right at the corner of Hyde Park to leave the city by Edgware Road. Buildings and crowds gave way to fields, common, and heathland, and to the east the distant villages of Highgate and Hampstead could just be made out on the horizon.

They trudged past the Chapel Street tollgate. On both sides of Edgware Road flocks grazed around the increasingly sparse houses. The occasional coach clattered past them at great speed, eager to avoid the highwaymen rumored to be lying in wait along the thoroughfare. The only activities this morning, though, were families working their allotments, solitary fishermen, and a great many children, all of whom stopped their work and play to gaze at the waves of brown-skinned folk walking through their world.

When the ragged band sat down to rest, two old women dragging hoes approached them. Buckram let one of them feel his skin and hair. The crones walked off to a small stone house from which they reappeared with a sack of apples and a bucket of water. The men drank and ate greedily as other villagers clustered round them to touch their flesh and joke with them.

Someone said, "Oooooo, innit lovely!" and everyone turned their faces to the southwest where three paddled hot-air balloons, one turquoise, one crimson, and one silver, were rising into the still, cloudless sky above Hyde Park.

This was the strangest island, Buckram thought. He tracked the balloons flying over his head and away to the hills.

The country itself had a different face and feel. His native land was one of aromatic woods: white cedar, maple, and pine. Here all the trees seemed stunted and scentless: the ash, the oak, the mulberry. The plant life was modest, as if God had gardened with a timorous touch.

He recognized a few flowers pushing through the new

spring grass: rye, dandelion, ribgrass, and timothy. An old brown mare was watching him from a crest in the meadow and his heart leapt as he saw it canter toward him.

He started to articulate what he believed was the horse-tongue taught him by a wandering Iroquois. But he realized his memory was failing and, instead, he was half-recalling one of Neville's biblical rants: "...he paweth in the valley...rejoiceth in his strength...goeth on to meet the armed man and is not affrighted...the glory of his nostrils is terrible...it sayeth amongst the trumpets, ha, ha!"

Age and ill-use had bleached the beauty from the beast. She coughed and snorted fine phlegm over Buckram's hair. Her coat sported scruffy patches, she had protruding ribs, and a thick, yellow discharge clogged her nostrils and eyes.

Buckram twisted fistfuls of grass from the earth, careful to avoid the foxgloves and ragwort. He rubbed the horse with it from mane to shoulder then combed her poll and forelock with his gnarly fingers. He stroked the mare once more and offered her the last of his apple.

"Buckram! Come, we're away!" Julius was calling him from the rear of the beggars' cortege as it shambled off down the road to Lisson Grove.

"Fare thee well, my friend," sighed Buckram, chucking the Thoroughbred under the chin. The horse whinnied and waggled her head. "Fare thee well."

He loped off to catch up with his fellow paupers, and when he looked back he saw one of the old girls who'd taken pity on them reining back the animal by her mane. The mare had been trying to follow him.

The woman laughed and patted the horse with surprising vigor. She hollered at Buckram, "Oooh, aren't you a lucky

Chimney-chops! Don't you know? He that's followed by a mare shall soon meet maiden sweet and fair!"

The horse neighed a final goodbye and Buckram found himself chuckling along the worn, dusty road.

They made it into Lisson Grove just before midday. The hamlet was full of poor, black men speaking strange English and alien tongues. As well as African-looking people, there were a number of East Indians and South Sea Islanders. Buckram paused to greet a Mohawk in his own language before shuffling on toward the public house where their six-penny stipend would be issued in an hour or so.

All of them, all three hundred or more of them, smelled as bad as Buckram knew he did. The crowd was thickest toward the door of the Yorkshire Stingo. Apart from a small, nervous-looking group of hussars sur-rounding the pub, there was not a white face to be seen. Buckram had never been among so many anxious, agi-tated black men in one spot in his life. Hungry black men were everywhere.

Suddenly he was seized by a delirious vision of this land, this London, in time to come, teeming with generation after generation of his kinfolk—freedmen English-born and bred—transforming this wet, cold island with African wor-ship and celebration. Imperial orphans in communion with a fractured past—his present—leading Albion's masses to a greater, more wholesome dance of life. Or would they, like him, still be hovering by closed doors, waiting for scraps from the master's table? And would they, like him, still be able to rely on the kindness of curious suburban strangers? God willing, death would find him before either of those futures came to pass.

He stumbled here and there, through the crowds of his people, waiting for his dole.

"Buckram!" The shout pierced through his reverie. "Buckram! Ethiopian Royal! Warrior, comrade!" It was a voice from the past, sailing over the heads of his fellow sadblacks. A voice from America. The voice of a friend. William Supple.

Buckram swiveled wildly in the throng, trying to locate the source of happy alarm in the hubbub.

"Over here, Buckie! Over here!"

William was standing on tiptoe in a trap driven by an utterly bewildered cabbie who had just found himself in the middle of this chaos.

Buckram, bearded head in the air, let himself be guided by William's voice to the expensive transport in which his oldest, truest friend stood. The two men embraced on the step of the open carriage.

"Man, you stink like a Billingsgate fishwife!" William held his old comrade away from him, staring with disbelief at what he saw. "What in God's name has happened to you? I saw George this morning...he said you were back, the old bastard...Buckram, we thought you dead, we thought... what have they done to you? Two years!"

Oblivious to the reeking humanity around him, the muttered curses of the driver, his friend's embarrassment, and the fleas under his two-year-old clothes, Buckram sobbed into the chest of the man he'd dragged from the battlefields of Carolina all those years ago, when they'd compared lashes and brandings and plotted revenge in that other world across the sea.

"Let's go home, Buckie. Forget this place. It's no good for

you. I've some money, and your old sword-pistol, remember that? I'll get you new clothes. You could use a good bath, believe me. We're going home. Come."

William settled his friend into the carriage. As they rattled away he was sure he heard someone behind them shouting for Buckram. He turned in his seat. A large, jovial-looking man was bouncing up and down in the road, waving both arms at the departing vehicle.

"Someone you know?" William inquired.

Buckram followed his gaze. There was Julius Bambara flapping about on the edge of the crowd, trying to attract their attention. Even from a distance, Buckram could read his lips. "Wait! Take me with you. Buckram, wait for me! Wait for me!"

"No, Willie," said Buckram. "Never seen him before in my life."

The driver whipped his way toward Edgware Road. And all the way back to the metropolis, Buckram realized: "This is home: London. This is my home: London. My friends are here. My life is here, and I live in this, our home: London town."

London, July 1783

It had been a thirsty summer for the beggars when Buckram first met Georgie George. A rumor had grown that black people could pass on fatal diseases simply by being in the vicinity of fresh, running water. As a result, watersellers avoided them and they were stoned and chased away from wells.

He had been lurking along the Strand one afternoon, scanning the throng for someone weaker to overpower, when he noticed a black man leaning against a well, laughing with a desperate-looking group of white people. He was short and he wore a frayed, navy blue frock coat. Mischievous eyes twinkled in an otherwise innocuous face.

The well stood on a crossing in the middle of the road, and horses, standing still in the noisy traffic, nibbled at its tiny green and bumped heads over a trough. The black man at the well drew up a ladle and drank in gulps. He passed on the half-empty ladle. Everyone spoke with familiarity and ease. The frock-coated man chortled and turned away. Buckram trailed him, watching him weave off round Fountain Court and zigzag into some nameless alley. He lost him some turnings on and stopped to locate himself. He found he was in a hilly street leading down to a timberyard on the Thames. He'd never been here and the area seemed even more run-down than St. Giles. Rats skipped freely from doorway to doorway and, at the bottom of the narrow slope, he could see mudlarks and other scavengers playing on logs piled by the riverfront. Barges and ferries moved across the sliver of river framed by tenements and lines of soot-flecked laundry.

A band of in-laws were shouting into each other's faces. Sunlight baked the neighborhood and the place reeked of gin.

"Oi, blackie!" The voice like a waterwheel was directly behind him. "What ye looking for in Dirty Lane?"

Buckram turned to warn off the speaker. He found he was facing the short black stranger. The man laughed, at first silently, then out aloud, clapping and hooting. Buckram's hand flew to his sword-pistol. He started to draw the blade but the man, though miming forgiveness, was still laughing. He let the sword slide back down the scabbard. The fool stopped laughing all too quickly and watched Buckram with the wary, intelligent stare of a man from the old colonies. A stare like his own.

"You're following me."

"Eh!"

"You've been stalking me from the Strand. Why?"

Buckram didn't reply.

The in-laws, detecting a harmonious voice, had postponed their brawl and were pointing at the outlanders inside their territory.

The frock-coated man grinned at them and waved inanely. They stopped in their tracks, blinking. Some made as if to wave back and some made puzzled sneers.

The black man feigned doffing a hat and bowing. A woman laughed in disbelief and all the children copied her. A hoarse voice bellowed, "Ballocks!" and the families broke into a charge.

"Let's go," the stranger commanded in the long vowels of the land of their birth.

Buckram saw how Georgie let targets approach him; how he sat out his mornings on a bench in St. James Park, then ambled by the stables at Charing Cross, before tripping up the Strand to the Piazza. He stopped off frequently in drinking dens and chophouses where he told tall stories and was offered beers and spirits in return.

Georgie also seemed to spend a lot of time passing messages from one set of street people to another. Jewelry and small statues were offered for his appraisal wherever he went. He carried very little money, yet Buckram saw him sealing several transactions involving vast sums with nothing but a handshake.

On a number of occasions he fell in beside prosperous citizens and spoke to them as they walked, seemingly picking up from earlier conversations. He'd bid them farewell a few corners on and return to the waiting Buckram with coins and notes he'd been given.

"Y'see now?" he once declared, patting his purse. "What any propertied white man needs is a friend, that's all. They've no one to talk to, most of them, no one at all. Don't trust each other. Talk to themselves, poor souls. So I'm their friend. And this is mine." He folded a note and put it in the torn seam of his coat.

"And this," he said as he flourished a second note, "this

is yours if you fall in with me. I'll wager you've got friends, old Carolina hands, old soldiers, good fighters, men-at-arms. We can use your sort in the Blackbirds."

Buckram wanted to know more.

"Let's just call it our little society. You've probably seen us round St. Giles. Doing work on behalf of the Black Poor, as a gentleman such as yourself might say. Join us, bring your buckos. I'll teach you everything you'll need to know. Everything."

Georgie was friends with everyone. Buckram saw how he seduced and obscured, then cajoled and spoke true. His was an incomparable world, as William described it: easy and busy, borderline but safe. His passion was in having the time of his life and nothing and no one could slight his desire.

The road to organized crime was a sharp, sweet drop. At first Buckram and William fenced for fences. They were pimps and lookouts and couriers. Sometimes they helped with coining—they learned how to drill and load dice and all the names for the different weightings; before long they could tell a bale of bard cinque deuces from a bale of direct contraries, and a bale of flat cater trees from a bale of langrets contrary to the ventage. They acquired the more arcane skills of pickpocketry from Elder Cadgers: the wipe-snitch, the cry-fake, the kinchin-lay, and how to nim a ticker. Specialists abounded: upright men, anglers, jarkmen, clank nappers, bufe nabbers, bilkers, fraters, and swaddlers and the climber damber himself, Georgie George. It was a fairly undemanding life compared to the hand-to-mouth existence they'd led hitherto. There was no shortage of food. All kinds of beers and spirits flowed freely and soon became part of their daily lives. Except for Neville, they ditched their fraying uniforms and started to buy new clothes—William especially. He quickly adopted the flamboyant dress code of their new circle of friends (the Blackbirds favored bright primary colors worn in combinations that would have clashed against white skins). The room in Ivy Street soon acquired mattresses, a cupboard, and a table. William gained membership at several gaming houses for gentlemen and he began, with little success, to apply himself to the theatrical arts.

The only hindrance to their new life was Pastor Neville. Georgie had taken an instant dislike to him and the feeling was mutual. Neville refused to partake in any illegalities and, on the one occasion when he visited the Charioteer, he was forcibly evicted after insisting on reading from the Book of Leviticus. He was a good bud nonetheless, and Buckram and William couldn't bring themselves to abandon him. The three of them had endured so much together and besides, he was the only good cook among them.

Gang life suited Buckram. The noisy, carefree atmosphere of the Charioteer was the ideal place for him to practice his gift of tomfoolery. It became his second home; in a matter of weeks he had gained enough status to merit the honor of a personal chair from which to conduct his business. He genuinely enjoyed Georgie's company—indeed everyone did—and took to accompanying the Beggar King as often as possible on his trips out to out-of-the-way villages like Tottenham and Camberwell.

One hot afternoon Georgie turned up at Ivy Street.

Buckram was alone waiting to interview an apprentice fellatrice from Hull. The room was unusually neat; the mattresses had been piled up, one on top of the other. The bare floorboards were swept clean and the pots and pans had been left in the keeping of the Igbo men downstairs.

Georgie was carrying a small tea chest. He dropped it on the floor and exhaled loudly. "Aieee! Heavy load, Buckie. Heavy load!"

Buckram stared nervously at the crate, appraising its weight.

"What've you got in there?" he asked hesitantly.

From inside the box came scratches and squeaks.

"A little investment." Georgie ground his teeth as he surveyed the room's dimensions. "Security against future losses."

"What's in the box, Georgie?"

Georgie flapped his frock coat then whipped out a handkerchief to mop his face. "Got any water, Buckie? I've a cruel thirst."

Dissimilar types of sharp claws poked out from opposite sides of the tea chest where tiny breathing holes had been punched out. The box rocked and wobbled.

"This is a rookery. Water's in the yard. Georgie, what is that? I mean, what sort of animal have you brought to my house?"

"Animalsss! A dog and a bird. Open it up. Have a look."

"Listen, I'm busy. I'm expecting company."

"Ah-hah! Hullside Harriet!" Georgie groaned appreciatively.

"Georgie, is this important?"

"As important as your life. You're looking at fifty pounds there."

"Fifty pounds of what?"

"Our money."

"Our...?!" Buckram gestured at the tea chest as if willing it to talk.

"It'll be three to two." Georgie tapped the box. "Twenty pounds is yours if you take care of our little friends here just till the weekend. Come on, open up the box. Have a look."

"You open it."

Georgie shook his head and muttered, "My God, black people, tsk-tsk-tsk." He worked a penknife under the lid and levered it off.

"This," he declared as he pulled out a torn, tightly tied sack with a beast wriggling within, "this is a guard dog from Imperial China." The animal shrieked.

"She dances too," Georgie added. "And this," a second ripped sack was extracted. "This is a prizefighter. Cock of the walk. No finer bird in the Court End. Want to see them?" Georgie began to loosen the drawstrings.

"No, no, I'll take your word for it. What am I supposed to do with them, anyway?"

The cock clucked and flapped.

"Look after them for a few days. Feed them. Let them run around some."

"Run around? You mad? This is Ivy Street. You can't keep a chicken here. It'll end up in some Jamaican's pot."

"Look, just keep them here for me. You're good with animals. You'll know what to do. It's twenty pounds, remember."

"I don't know, George. I don't know. Where they from, anyway?"

"Pete Fortune. Some of his buckos visited the Red Lion last night and, errm, took charge of the beasties in lieu of payment for a debt. Landlord's got till the weekend to come up with the money."

"You mean the ransom?"

"Whatever. Just help out, eh? Be a bud."

"Dunno. For two days maybe."

"Three days," prompted Georgie, starting to smile.

"I'll have to ask the others."

"Done." Georgie rubbed his hands and wiped his face. "Aren't you going to have a look at your new lodgers?"

"Later, after Harriet has passed through. There are fleas aplenty in this place as it is."

"Yesss," agreed Georgie absently. "In abundance." He stepped up to the window. The broken pane was stuffed with material torn from an old pair of breeches. He ran a forefinger along the sill and examined the layers of dust. "This is a shit hole," he stated. "You're Blackbirds now. You should set an example."

Buckram almost laughed. "If you say so, George."

The Beggar King looked out of the window. A ball game was in progress in the courtyard; four scruffy men, one Lascar, one white, and two blacks were slapping a ball against a wall.

He frowned. "Oh, oh, here comes company."

Buckram joined him at the window and watched as the ball players stopped their game to allow a couple access to the building. It was Harriet and Neville.

She was a fat, pretty woman with badly dyed blonde hair. Even without her high heels she would have stood at six feet and one inch.

"Big girl!" whooped Georgie.

"See me running?" countered Buckram.

"What's the preacher doing with her? Showing her the straight and narrow?"

"God knows. He's the last person I need to see right now." Buckram ran his fingers through his hair and went to hunt for his wig.

"Well." Georgie clapped his hands. "I'll be on my way. I'll call by this evening with some seed and butcher's scraps. And whatever you do, don't go shouting about this." He flicked a nod at the two jumping sacks. "You have a good time, yes?"

Buckram walked him to the door. He hung over the landing and followed Georgie as the Beggar King negotiated the steps in semidarkness. He heard him yell a single word of greeting to Harriet and cough a curt bark at Neville.

Silence fell as Neville and Harriet moved up the stairs.

Buckram pulled Harriet through the door with one hand while holding Neville at the threshold with the other.

"I found this woman lost in Phoenix Street," the preacher explained. "She claimed knowledge of you, so I brought her here." He leaned forward and whispered, "She's a bawd, you know. I can tell."

"Neville, I thank you for your help and your observations, but the young lady and I need to be alone." Buckram started to close the door.

The dog howled and Neville started.

"What was that?" he asked, peeking over Buckram's shoulder.

"Nothing. It's nothing. Nothing to worry about."

Pastor Neville scowled and shook his head. "Thou shalt not bring the hire of a whore, or the price of a dog, into the house of the Lord thy God…"

"Goodbye, Neville!"

"I think not," said Neville and brushed past his friend to join Harriet in the room. She was kneeling in the corner, poking at the sacks with a parasol.

"Awhhh, it's a little doggie," remarked Harriet. "Let's have a look."

"No!" Buckram shouted.

The cock began to crow.

"Release them," ordered Neville. "Why are the beasts so bound?"

Buckram grabbed Neville by the lapels and dragged him back out onto the landing. "My friend, this is business. I'll not have it ruined by your folly. Go now!"

"I will not," protested Neville. "For every creature of God is good and nothing to be refused if it be..."

Buckram shoved the preacher down the stairs. He raced back to the room and locked the door.

Harriet was scampering merrily around the mattresses in pursuit of the dog, who was chasing the chicken.

"What are you doing?!?" he screamed.

"They're playing. Awhhh, look at 'em. They're playing."

It took them twenty minutes to separate the animals, re-sack them and fling them in the cupboard. They howled and crowed and knocked and whined behind the flimsy doors. They kept up the fuss throughout Buckram and Harriet's hour-long "interview."

Buckram saw his new worker down to the street and left her with instructions for her first shift. She would do well, he thought, tugging at his waistband. He could see that he'd have to review her progress on a regular basis. He dawdled in the courtyard, basking in the envy of his sex-starved neighbors.

There was commotion in the street. Five white men, deep in heated conversation, stepped up to the courtyard. Two of them were Charlies, one looked like a man of substance, the other two were clearly nothing but thugs.

"This the place?" asked one Charlie.

"It is, in very deed," replied the rich man.

"You there!" The Charlie singled out Buckram. "D'you live here?"

Buckram shrugged his shoulders. "No speak English," he said. He snuck back into the house while the others on the street were being questioned in sign language—the Charlie made dog and chicken noises.

Buckram had to get rid of the animals. He scurried into his room and opened the cupboard. The cock had scratched its way out of its sack and through the dog's sack, and was now blinking innocently over a mess of bloodied fur, eyeballs, and blue silk ribbon.

"Ogod!"

The bird preened, flapped its wings, puffed up its chest and sang, "Cock-a-doodle-doo! Cock-a-doodle-doo!"

The Charlies were breaking down his door by the time he'd kicked the chicken to death.

Buckram was beaten and dragged to Bow Street for the first night of seven hundred and thirty that he would spend behind bars.

London, 30 May 1786

William counted the stairs as he climbed up through the darkness with a tankard full of porter...fifteen...sixteen...seventeen. Stepping carefully over the two missing steps he stood on the tiny landing and felt for the padlocks.

His room was a garret above the Coopers' Arms. In the basement the last few customers were leaving the cockpit and filing up to the ground-floor bar.

He opened the door, put the tankard on the floor, and collapsed onto a large, brass double bed. As he relaxed, the pain in his right side reawakened. He lay staring up at patterns washing across his ceiling from the lamps across the alley at the Lemon Tree.

As he rolled onto his stomach, the pain redoubled. He reached for a bottle of opium and licorice cordial on the bedside table. He swallowed seven-eighths of it and rolled onto his back again.

Drinkers from the Lemon Tree were coming out into the alley, singing lewd limericks in its double echo. The light dance on the ceiling seemed to move in time to their voices. Listening to the lyrics, William felt the narcotic bleeding through his stomach walls and being sucked up in his blood, turning his spine to crystal fire.

> *There was a new maid from Drury*
> *The toast of all London Jewry*
> *For one day she surmised*
> *That the uncircumcised*
> *Made more healthy, more wealthy*
> *One-twoery*

He tracked the drug's thousand fingers searching for his discomfort, locating it, closing in, closing it down.

When he felt sufficiently healed he stepped across the green Axminster carpet and opened his wardrobe. He took out a fresh white shirt and threw his blood-stained one on a pile of dirty clothes in the corner. He washed his upper body over a porcelain bowl with the same greasy water he'd brought up from the bar last night. He smudged dust off his hat and waistcoat with a wet rag.

He lit a lantern and looked in the mirror. Bruised, sunken eyes, sparsely haired head, mostly gray curls. His oyster-colored teeth matched his oyster-colored gums. His face showed an age of one hundred and seventeen and he looked older than Samuel, or Gullah, as his surrogate father back in Carolina on Blackstock's Plantation preferred to be called.

When he'd finished changing he went to a bookshelf and took out a copy of Ignatius Sancho's *Letters*. He opened it at page twenty-three and slipped out ten pounds for himself and one for Georgie. After angling the lantern away from the freshly painted wall, he blew out the flame and walked to the door.

He'd lived alone in Rose Street for almost one-and-a-half years now, and he loved the peace in his home, so he'd felt a weight off his mind when he heard that Buckram had decided to stay with Neville.

Seeing him again had been a disaster. Buckram was in a critical state of disconnection; he had become a lunatic. William thought about his children back in Charleston, South Carolina or who knows where, or who knows whose. They'd called him "Uncle Buckram." How'd they like to see their uncle now?

Of all the old fighters who'd made it to England, Buckram had been the one least likely to go under. His constitution had always been incredible and his sense of humor was legendary. During the spring campaign of 1781, when all the frontline troops were going down with Saint Anthony's fire, smallpox, and strangury, Buckram was afflicted with only a mild head cold and "rising of the lights." He could always be relied on to cancel out melancholy and sidestep seriousness. Even on the approach to battle, marching forward to replace fallen comrades, he'd be quick-ripping and oafing it up.

Once a military tribunal found him guilty of "skylarking" and awarded him fifty lashes. Later, when he retold the story—as he often did—his eyes would swell with touching pride at his crime. Buckram: skylarker. It was official.

The day Buckram finally shipped out of New York, leaving William and Mary to fend for their children in the beleaguered port, had been the second worst day of William's life. He knew he'd lost his guardian angel.

Almost a year later and alone in London, he stumbled upon his friend in Henrietta Street. Buckram was slumped on a building site, sharing a bottle of rotgut with a rag-shod bunch of African sailors.

William had just moved to Ivy Street, and he insisted that Buckram and Neville leave Ratcliffe immediately—too close to the docks, too convenient for slave-raiding parties—and come over to the more metropolitan squalor of St. Giles.

Good times soon came round again for the three old cronies. Buckram was a skillful thief and footpad, and Neville was a resourceful cook. Having them around seemed to boost William's luck and his gambling career took off with some measure of success.

They began to frequent the Charioteer and eventually came to be accepted among the better-heeled galaxy of black villains that made up the merry, malevolent London of Georgie George.

Buckram vanished soon after that, in the course of some madcap spree with the Beggar King. The whole parish knew that Georgie was implicated in his disappearance but, as usual, nothing could be proved.

William resolved then and there to lead a single life. And this he had done to his satisfaction until twelve hours ago, when Buckram resurfaced, changed beyond all recognition.

If this city could break a soul like Buckram's, how much more easily could it annihilate his own?

William settled himself beside Georgie on a wall bench at the Golden Cross Inn in Charing Cross and ordered a jar of Rhenish wine.

The Cross was the stopping-off place for coaches arriving from the south coast and the west country. It was always full of European tourists and wide-eyed shire folk in the capital for the first time. And Georgie was a friend of the landlord, of course.

It was a white man's pub where they knew they could relax, being more seasoned Londoners than most of the clientele. Few of them had ever seen black humans before and it amused the two ex-slaves to pass the odd evening in this tavern, telling lies and sponging drinks.

They had been toasted as Princes of Araby, Lords of Ethiopia, Malian potentates, and ambassadors from Benin. Masquerading as traditional healers, they had sold fishing flies and dried herbs as cures for gonorrhea and scurvy. And on quite a few occasions Georgie had walked out of the door with a woman on his arm.

After two years in London it still amazed William how Georgie could do that. With a white woman. In a white man's country. And live.

"You're still looking rough, Billy-boy. What's got you?"

William unbuttoned his shirt and showed George his bandages. "I took a drubbing last night. While you were out gallivanting with that South London crew."

Georgie tut-tutted. "You should choose your friends more carefully, William. A man is judged by the company he keeps. Now, since you started prancing round the Court End, dancing attendance on gentry and calling yourself an actor, people take to you differently."

He wagged a finger under William's nose. "No one in this town likes to see a fancy black man. Especially a poor white man with seven children and one shirt. You've forgotten that. Hmmm?"

William uncrossed then recrossed his arms as Georgie poured wine for them both.

"Y'see," Georgie continued, "you'd never find yourself in like trouble when you used to run with St. Giles's Blackbirds. You'd have been in there, like the rest of us, clapping heads and taking a rightful cut of the booty."

"Georgie, that was a riot last night. There was no plan to what happened. They were attacking anyone."

Georgie just gave him one look and shook his head. "What sort of mushrooms are you eating? You're sounding like those fools down the road." He flicked his head toward the Palace of Westminster.

"I'm not like you, Georgie. I couldn't live in a jail. I'd crack the walls; I'd see the other side in there. Like Buckram."

Georgie spun a crown on the table. It twirled straighter and faster than a child's top until it stopped, standing still.

William gazed at the trick, mesmerized.

"Oh. Buckram," said Georgie. "I often wondered why he used to laugh so much. He was just too wild. Like that night he jumped Bannie and gave him a beating in the middle of Russell Street!"

William laughed, recalling the look of pure terror on the face of Banastre Tarleton, their old commanding officer. They had spotted the hard-faced, effeminate man leaving Chapman's Coffeehouse in Bow Street; he was parting company with a raucous, overdressed fop and an even louder painted lady.

"That's the Prince of Wales he's with," said Georgie, "and that's his mistress, the actress Mary Robinson."

William asked how he knew this and Georgie nonchalantly informed him that they were both good friends of his. They trailed Tarleton to the Piazza. Buckram had called out to him, "Hey, Bannielad, looking for cunny? Step over here! I've got something for you."

Finding himself surrounded by four blacks, Tarleton drew his sword. William and Georgie carried razors, Henry Prince wielded a short, heavy meat cleaver, and Buckram was leveling his sword-pistol at Sir Banastre's genitals.

"It's loaded," he said. "So drop your sword, then your purse, and begone, murderer."

Sir Banastre obeyed the first part of the order but then Buckram barred his way.

"We're not finished with you yet. Some of us were with you for that massacre at Waxhaws. You remember the children in the schoolhouse, don't you? Don't you!?!"

He kicked him in the thigh.

"Well, some of us worked with the gang on burial duty."

None of them, William, Neville, or Buckram, would ever forget what they were asked to dispose of that day: cupboards full of decapitated heads, corpses halved and corpses quartered, and that still-dying, disemboweled woman clawing feebly at the air. On the barn walls above her written in blood were the words "Thou shalt never give birth to a rebel."

"I remember you now," Tarleton lied. "You were all good boys back then. Stout fellows. Well done."

"Stop your foolishness!"

Buckram slapped him in the chest with the flat of his sword, pushed him over, and stamped all over his body.

"Thanking you for the wages, sirrah. Better late than never."

Buckram pocketed the purse. When they opened it, round the corner in Brydges Street, they counted close to thirty pounds. They trooped into the Soup Shop Ale House to begin a week-long session of drinking and whoring.

"Yes," said Georgie. "Something bad was always on the cards for him, sooner or later. How d'you think he's doing?"

"Who can say? I went over to the Stingo today and found him waiting with all the beggars, just like you said he'd be. He's living with Neville by the church. I don't know what'll become of him now. I gave him some money and a few clothes and sent him round to Jack the Jamaican in Ivy Street for a bit of barbering. Can't believe what's happened to him."

"He told you I'd offered him some work?"

"Work? You think Buckie'll want to throw in with you again, after the first time? You're mad!"

"Depends how desperate he gets. Times are getting tougher for beggars and sadblacks. They say the Charlies are hunting them down, rounding them up."

"Nonsense. That's impossible. There'll always be blacks begging in London. That's how it was long before us and that's how it'll be long after we're gone."

"Well, I'm only telling you what I hear. But you don't work the streets anymore. You wouldn't know how it is. You spend too much time alone in that nice room of yours. A woman's touch is what you need."

William looked at him sharply. "I've got a woman. And a family!"

"Oh yes, of course. Mary and the boys. It can't be easy. You must think of them often."

"Not much." William scratched his nose. "Every day."

"Oh, by the way," said Georgie, reaching into his pocket, "I picked up a little something for your dear lady. What d'you think?" He handed William a tiny, ornate, silver box. William lifted the lid. A barely audible air from "London Bridge Is Falling Down" tinkled from its interior. On the lid was an engraved inscription: "To Mary, Thy auburn locks are more lovely in my sight than golden beams of orient light. Your loving William."

"It's lovely," gasped William, pondering the reference to "auburn locks." "Where'd you get it from?"

"Y'know," said Georgie. He held out his palms. "These things come my way now and again. It's the sort of thing a young lady would appreciate, don't you think?"

"Why, yes. Surely. Thanks, Georgie."

He felt as cold and restless as the ocean that separated him from his kin. He steadied himself with more drink and read, for maybe the hundredth time, a printed Act of Parliament nailed to the tavern wall, which advised against drinking, swearing, and all manner of profanities. He took another gulp of wine and snapped down the lid on the box.

"A question," said Georgie. "Tell me, what would you do if you had two thousand pounds? Where would you go with that sort of money? As a black man, I mean."

William didn't have to think. "I'd fulfill my promise to my family. We'd be together again as freemen. We'd start a new life."

"But where?"

"We'd go to Nova Scotia and start a farm. Like I should have done in the first place."

Georgie shook his head. "You? On a farm in Canada?

No. That's an even colder, whiter country than this. And you're no backwoodsman. Look at you. Living the life of a gentlemen," he snorted.

"Happy as a pig in shit. Fancy friends, fancy food, fancy wine. If you were given the chance, wouldn't you bring your family out here? You do seem to love it so."

William found he could not answer, so he read the act one more time, opened the music box, and sang the words to the tune under his breath.

London, 20 June 1786

Buckram walked up and down Drury Lane till he saw a number that matched the one Georgie had written out for him: 66.

He paused to brush dust from the clean set of clothes he'd borrowed from William: the brown, double-breasted waistcoat with the square-cut hem and a yellow standing collar, the hard-wearing, blue workshirt, the long, gunmetal breeches with ornamental ribbon garters, and small, square knee buckles, the white cotton stockings stuffed with calf-pads and the wooden-soled patten shoes. He straightened the rosette on his bicorne hat and braced his shoulders.

He walked through a narrow door and down a short flight of stairs to a wide, low-ceilinged workshop full of large printing presses, dirty oak cabinets, and cluttered bookshelves. An old man wearing lunettes approached him. His neck and shoulders were bent from long stooping.

"Peacock's, the printers?" Buckram inquired.

"The very same." The man wiped his hands on his apron. "A good morning to you, sir. How may I be of assistance?"

"My name is Buckram. I've come to collect the order for Mr. Prince of Exeter Street."

"Ah-hah, an emissary from the Black Prince. The Ethiopian literature, I take it?"

"The books with the black whores in them, yes."

"Right you are, sir. One moment, if you please."

He sloped away to unlock a little cabinet.

"And how many will sir be requiring?"

"Twenty, or so, for now. I'll come back this afternoon if I need more."

The old man handed Buckram a loose bundle of the sealed papers. "An excellent collection, if you don't mind me saying, sir. Quite the fashion, these days, those young blacks."

Buckram wondered why he replied, "Thank you."

He got to the Piazza just as the morning market was at its height. Local women washed clothes and children at the pump while exchanging insults with costermongers and porters.

Across the Piazza were the Turkish baths—the Hummums—where Neville had taken him for his first wash after his release. He'd spent nearly four shillings of his friend's money luxuriating for almost an entire night in the steam rooms and having his skin scraped by a giant with a camel-hair rag. Strumpets were also available as part of the house service, but he refused the offer, seeing as he was there at Neville's behest. He didn't need a woman like that anyway. There'd been women aplenty in jail.

He maneuvered through fruit and flower stalls to stand by the wall of St. Paul's Church where caged larks and lin-nets were on sale.

It occurred to him that he hadn't the first idea how to sell books. As usual, Georgie had told him nothing and was nowhere to be found. How would the Beggar King handle this situation?

Who at this time of day would be looking for "Aethiopian Cyprians"? Almost any rich, white man newly arrived in town, he decided. There were precious few of those to be found in the market, so he wound his way over to the Piazza Hotel. It was a bawdy house-cum-hotel frequented, almost exclusively, by country squires. He positioned himself by an arch in front of the entrance and waited.

Five minutes elapsed before the first resident came through the door. An overly short, middle-aged man with yellow-white hair, badly cut, exited onto the Piazza, looking left and right, as if hoping not to be recognized. Precisely the sort of gentleman for whom attracting female company was a problem. Buckram sidled up to the prospect, brandishing his texts like an oversized decks of cards.

"Good day, sir!" he exclaimed. "New in town? Seeking exotic delights?"

The man examined him with mounting, quizzical rage. When he harrumphed Buckram realized just how big a mistake he had made. The noise the mark had produced was one that no Englishman could have emitted. No European either, for that matter. Buckram asked another question. "Would it be business or pleasure that brings you to this fair city, sir?"

"That," the man replied, "that is not something I am prepared to discuss with one of your hue. Distance yourself, nigger, lest I have you flogged for insolence."

White American.

Voice dark and slurred like molasses. Eyes heavy and

gray as a Boston shower. Someone who could deflower black virgins at will. Someone who could have once owned him.

Buckram held the planter's gaze, feeling confident and comfortable with the anger building inside him.

"I don't think you heard me, boy. Stand aside, I say."

But Buckram stood akimbo, blocking his path.

"Where do you hail from, slave owner?"

The American drew back his arm. Before the fist could fly Buckram grasped it with his own, twisted his wrist, and slammed him against a pillar.

A gaggle of onlookers was gathering, so Buckram raised his voice and spoke London English for all to hear.

"I asked where you came from, rebel. Answer me!"

The man's nostrils flared. He looked to the crowd for support, but they were all passing fops and St. Giles's toughs, eager for a fight to staunch their boredom.

"Are you going to let this nigger defy me? Will you allow him to besmirch the honor of the white…!"

Buckram cuffed him across the mouth; his knuckles felt teeth loosen in the gums.

"Dob 'im one on, blackie! Dob 'im one on for the lads!" came a plaintive voice from the crowd.

Buckram's ruse had worked. The crowd was siding with him. The American, realizing this, squealed like a Smithfield pig and sagged to his knees, cupping his bloody mouth with his hands.

"Where's home, rebel? Where's home?"

"Camden, Carolina."

"Ah, Camden," Buckram declared. "Know it well. Spent a good time there during your war against our king."

The market folk warmed to this mention of shared sovereignty.

"Camden. Fine little town. Swived many a young lass there. Me and my fellow blacks. Mayhap your wife or daughter was of their number."

"Ooooh!?!" smarmed the Londoners.

The American gathered up the vestiges of his dignity and spat blood in the ex-slave's face.

Buckram grabbed him by the scruff of his neck and presented him to the crowd.

"You see these colonials. See them? This is the gratitude we get for trying to save their filthy hides from the folly of independence. This is how they repay us. Take that!"

He punched the planter in the stomach.

"That's for Boston!"

"Woooaaargh!" went the audience.

He clapped the man's left ear as hard as he could. He felt the impact resound through his tightened muscles. "That's for Philadelphia!"

"We're with you, darkie!"

"That's for Savannah!" He held him up and hiked his knee into his crotch.

Three more cities on the Atlantic seaboard were mentioned before it dawned on Buckram that this was the least satisfying beating he had ever dealt. He dropped his crumpled enemy on the ground and stamped off through a gauntlet of laughing cheers.

A drunkard clutched at his sleeve and began to make declarations of undying friendship. Buckram shrugged him off and made his way out of the Piazza.

If he'd had a knife, he'd have turned back and cut out the

man's heart. The crowd would have welcomed that, he knew. Covent Garden was that kind of place, but he felt disgusted with his performance and quick-marched up James Street, trying to outdistance his shame.

Outside the Nag's Head a young black beggar, still a child and obviously a runaway, skipped up to him with hands outstretched. The boy danced around him, moaning and barking. Collar marks had bruised his neck, his lips had been cut off, and when he opened his mouth Buckram saw that he was tongueless. He had no money to give the child and gestured as much. The beggar bowed and curtsied before spiraling away to his haunt at the tavern's dog porch.

Buckram sighed with exasperation and leaned against the corner of Hart Street. He removed his hat and wiped the sweatband with his forefinger.

He was staring glumly at the ludicrous booklets in his hands and wondering what on earth could have possessed him to buck up with Georgie again, when he caught a whiff of a familiar fragrance. It was a smell like a handful of warm raisins, a scent that he hadn't inhaled in a long time. An unperfumed black woman had passed by and he was in her wake.

He saw her hurrying down Hart Street. She wore a deep-bodiced, closed sable gown with plain, short-cuffed, elbow-length sleeves. Unwigged hair was covered with a large cap and her skirt was draped up toward the back to reveal a neatly blanched underpetticoat.

An unescorted woman of quality.

She was bidding shopkeepers good afternoon and ignoring the coarse calls of barrow boys.

He trailed her to the gates of the Adelphi School. She

stopped to rifle through the contents of her bag and he stopped too, five yards behind. Buckram felt his heartbeat pounding from somewhere near his throat as he diminished the space between them and came up to her side.

She flicked him a glance, then jumped back a full step. She had a sepia-colored, full vixen face and swift swallow eyes. Buckram gazed, stunned.

"Ma'am," he croaked, at a loss for what to say to make the moment continuous.

He doffed his hat—William's hat—and held it to his chest like a shield. Ease with women had long abandoned him. He straightened his spine and summoned what he could recall of gravitas.

"You seemed lost, sister. Perhaps you are unfamiliar with this area. I go by the name of Buckram, a resident here of long standing. With your permission, I'd be only too pleased to..."

She laughed in his face. A dolphin laugh: k-k-k-k-k-k-k. And that laugh seemed to embody all the self-assurance he couldn't muster.

"My brother," she'd replied (brother—good sign), "clearly you do not know of me." Her voice carried the strident, overconfident sonority of a freeborn black Briton.

"My name is Charlotte Tell and I am a teacher of mathematics and Latin at this venerable establishment." She gestured casually to the Free School's dowdy gates.

"I am very well-known throughout this parish and I fear it is you, rather than me, who is the stranger here."

She laughed again then dipped her gorgeous eyes back to her bag.

Buckram held his space, petrified, at her side, watching

her pull out quills and notes, watching her replace them. From time to time she looked back at him. Her eyes said, "Well?"

His said, "Well what?"

A bell rang over the tiny concession of cobbles that served as a schoolyard.

"Mr. Buckram." She smiled at him, as if humoring an infant. "I must go now. My class awaits within."

She did not move. Her eyes flashed up and down his body and she half-smiled.

"You are born of this land, are you not?" asked Buckram.

"As much as you are of yours. We are all black, wherever we are from, whatever we do. You're from the colonies, I can tell. A soldier."

Buckram hunched his shoulders, then let them fall. "I have no more fights," he muttered. "I just live in this world as best I can, ma'am."

She pointed to the manuscripts under his arm. "So, you're a writer, a diarist, a published scribe."

"...!"

"Have you read Phillis Wheatley? I took it that reading and writing were forbidden to our people in America."

The bell rang again.

"Errrm, that is true, tho' many of us can cipher as well as any white man. I carry here the work of a friend. Impressions of London. Its delights and perils."

Her face lit up, markedly erotic in its incandescence.

"Oh, how wonderful." She looked swiftly at the school-yard then back to Buckram. "May I see a copy?"

"A copy of this?" Buckram scratched his head and sensed

himself staring intently at her Oriental-style slipper shoes. "These books are for sale only."

"Oh, I see. Then perhaps you'd be so good as to deliver some examples of your friend's work to my home address."

Like most illiterates, Buckram had a terror of addresses but an excellent memory.

"I keep rooms at number 43 Long Acre, next door to the alehouse for sodomites, the Wheatsheaf. You must know it?"

Buckram pursed his lips. Everyone knew it.

"I can be found at home most evenings after five o'clock. Do send a copy round. Please. I'll be waiting. Good day."

She vanished into the schoolhouse before he could phrase a reply. Buckram stared dumbly at the spot where she'd stood, feeling goosebumps.

He walked back toward James Street, taking long, languid steps. He repeated the name Charlotte Tell; it danced on his tongue. He felt the swell of the afternoon sun as he turned the corner. And his only thought for the next hour and a half was: 43.

What did that look like?

London, 20 June 1786

The makeshift gambling board tilted precariously under a weight of drinks and coins. William Supple rolled a tiny whisky glass between his palms while waiting for the last of his five companions to show their hands. Ten or so other men, their games long finished, stood in silence around them, signaling wordless bets on the outcome.

They were playing in a small, brightly lit cellar under the Strand. The temperature in the gambling den was warmer than that on the surface and the men played in shirt-sleeves—their coats hung on the backs of their chairs. The air was filled with tobacco smoke and the smell of soil and old bricks.

William watched as Gerhard the Hessian studied his cards and stroked his great, red beard. The German was also a veteran of the colonial wars; his regiment had served with William's at a number of battles in the Carolina campaign and, like some of the black servicemen, he had chosen to make London his home.

They exchanged a brief look and—William thought—a conspiratorial smile. Gerhard drew a few coins from his purse and stacked them on the board. The company exhaled loudly.

"Ten shillings further, William," he whispered. "Will you meet me? I dare you."

William stared him full in the face and nodded. "Do your worst, Hessian."

The German spread his cards on the table, almost failing to mask his anxiety.

A king, a pair of nines, and the Jack of Hearts.

William willed himself expressionless as pockets of malevolent cheer erupted around him.

He fanned out his cards with quiet dignity: his Ace, his Queen of Hearts, his Jack of Diamonds, his Ten of Spades.

His victory.

He took some comfort in the overhearty applause from the fickle, fortune-hunting crowd. They'd come to cheer a winner.

And here he was, ever the actor.

"Outplayed again," admitted the Hessian. "Outplayed again."

A boy came over to clear away the glasses and take a cut for the house.

"You've a visitor, Mr. Supple. At the door. Wants to talk to you."

"Tell him I'm busy, Giles," said William, "and fetch us another round of usquebaugh." William gathered up the pack to shuffle a game of faro.

"It's a black man, sir." Giles raised his eyebrows and nodded significantly. "Goes by the name of Buckram. Says it's an urgency."

William sucked his teeth. "Tell him I'll be up in a minute."

He passed the pack to Gerhard and strutted to the door.

Three bolts were removed and two locks were turned before William could mount the steps to the street.

Buckram stood with hat—his hat—in hand. Warm, fresh air steamed in from the Strand and Buckram kicked his heels in the dark, dusty street.

"Hello, Buckie, how is it?"

"Oh, I'm not too bad. Sought you all over tonight, William. I need to talk to you about something. Whaddye' say we go sink a few jars down the Charioteer?"

With as much exasperation as he reckoned their friendship could stand, William started explaining how busy he was, making an illegal living down in the cellar, and that he was available to friends during daylight hours only.

It hurt him to say that. He'd taken such care to avoid Buckram these past weeks. Best to keep things superficial. Just thinking about the Charioteer was depressing.

A door opened down behind him and the servant boy shouted, "Table's ready and calling for you, Mr. Supple."

"Bid them wait!"

"Are you winning?" Buckram asked.

He was looking better, William noticed; the jailhouse edges blurred back toward normality, the haunted eyes were still haunted, but at home. He was a man at leisure, wanting to celebrate his liberty. The old Buckram. Maybe.

"Winning? Yes," William slowly replied. "I'll join you in a while."

He returned to the cellar to close his affairs with the house then bounded back up the stairs, pulling on his coat.

"Let's walk around for a bit. I need some air."

They strolled down to Charing Cross past small crowds of night people enjoying the antics of sword swallowers and a man lifting a four-hundred-pound weight with the hair of his head. William paused by a Gypsy girl who was goading a small dancing dog to gavotte. He noted Buckram frowning at the spectacle and reconsidered throwing her the coin he had palmed in his pocket.

With the exception of coal carts coming up from the river front and the odd horseman or sedan chair, the street was free of traffic and, like everyone else, William and Buckram walked along in the middle of it.

"How's your side?" inquired Buckram.

"No complaints. Hardly a war wound. I'm all right as long as Georgie keeps me supplied with this." He pulled a brown glass bottle from his pocket: opium cordial.

"He tells me," said William, "that you're working for him and Henry."

"Sort of. I sell prints and guides around the Piazza."

"Oh, I can imagine."

"No you can't. I was stopped by the Charlies in Southampton Row today. They asked me my business. Threatened to deliver me to the Navy Office if I didn't give them some money. I caught one of them on the jaw and had to run. I lost them in Clare Market, but I think they'll come looking for me, y'know. They'll remember my face."

William laughed openly. "No, Buckie, you're safe from the watch. Don't you know they can't tell one black man from another? You just have to lay low for a day or so, then resume your work. Stick to St. Giles and Seven Dials. They can't touch you there."

"I'm sick of the place. Sick of this town, William."

"But where else is there?"

"Sierra Leone."

"What?"

"Sierra Leone. Africa. You must have heard the news, seen the handbills, the posters. Everyone's talking about it."

"Well, I don't talk to everyone. Don't read too much nowadays either."

"So, you really don't know, do you? They're planning to clear us off the streets. They want us out of this country."

"And...?"

"Any black, or Lascar, found not working will be held at Newgate for transportation. They're making the White Raven beggars agree to sign for a place in their scheme before they receive their sixpence."

"Transportation to Africa? What the devil d'you mean? Every year they invent something new to scare us with. It never works. We're still here. There's too many of us, slaves, ex-slaves, freeborn and all, just too many. I read in *Gentleman's Magazine*..."

"*Gentleman's Magazine?*"

"...there are fifteen thousand of us in London alone. They'll have to call out the soldiers to take us on. It's impossible. It'll never happen."

"Wouldn't you like to go?"

"To Sierra Leone? No. I heard some old settlers from Nova Scotia talk about it. But that's a freeman's country, they can choose how and when they go. Over here it's different. Imagine the Englishman inviting us to return to Africa. We'd end up in chains, for sure."

He'd heard about the west coast of Africa and all he knew was that it attracted slavers like bees to a sugar plantation.

"You're happy here, aren't you?" asked Buckram.

William didn't answer.

They bought two portions of cold chicken pie with cat-sup from a street vendor in Villiers Street and sat down beside the Charing Cross pillory block to eat. In front of them loomed a statue of King Charles I on horseback. The starless sky was as clear as a London night could be.

"That's where I should look for work," said Buckram. He pointed to a filthy warren of long, low sheds over the crossing. It looked like a penal colony for dwarfs. The stench of horse manure was overwhelming. Distant whinnying and the clang of blacksmiths' hammers carried over to them.

"You'd never get a start in there," said William. "That's the King's Mews. They can't take black people."

"But that's my trade. Horseman. I won't live like a tramp again."

"You seem to be doing all right. My clothes look better on you than they do on me. You look to go a-courting."

"That's what I want to talk to you about."

"You've found a lady friend?"

"I'm not sure. I think so. Maybe."

William had never seen Buckram like this before, rendered speechless by a woman. He wanted to know more.

"Who is she?"

"I thought you might tell me. I don't know her. Just met her this afternoon. Young black woman, a teacher by the name of Charlotte Tell."

"The schoolmarm at the Adelphi School, Hart Street?"

"The same. D'you know her?"

William finished the last of his pie and slowly wiped crumbs and sauce from his lips.

"Oh, yes. Miss Tell. Everyone knows of her. She's a woman of some quality, y'know. Some quality."

"How d'you mean?"

"I mean that she's very well-connected, has independent means, and a mind of her own. She's a strange one."

"She's beautiful."

"Yes, she's very beautiful, but she's from another world."

"She was born here."

"Exactly. Her manners and graces aren't ours. She's more like the Sanchos or one of those Mayfair blacks you see from time to time."

"What can you tell me about her?"

"Well, her mother and father were brought over here as servants of the Earl of Stanford. He has a Jamaican estate y'know: sugar, rum. She was raised in his Staffordshire household as one of his own. She grew up with the Earl's children and was schooled into a young woman by private tutors. When the Earl died a year or so back, she came into a tidy bit of legacy and annuity. She moved down to London to be closer to her own kind, as most of them do in the end, y'know. She mixes with some political types, abolitionists, free radicals, and what have you. What I'm trying to say is that she's not of our caste in any way, shape, or form. She's practically a gentlewoman. You've taken to her, then?"

"I think so." Buckram nodded and—William thought—shivered.

William whistled. "Let's go for that drink."

They set off toward St. Martin's Lane.

"You should relax more, Buckram. With the women, I mean. Remember how you used to be?"

"Too well. But we were fresh out of the army. First time in London. Never been around white women before. Things have changed."

"What's changed?"

"I have. There's something I haven't told anybody. Things I did, things I was made to do in jail." He paused on the steps of the church and faced William.

"When I landed up in the Bridewell I was penniless. I couldn't afford to buy good food and drink from the turnkeys. They put me in a cell with nine other men. All white. All crazy. Some of them had been in there twelve years. We had a ration of thin gruel and hard bread, and we had to fight over it like wild dogs.

"Once or twice a week the turnkeys would throw a young girl in with us just to see what we would do to her. Some of those girls died, William. It was hell.

"Then one night they came for me and dragged me into a private room. This table they had, it was laden with roast goose and cheese, dry devils, French bread, and Hereford cider. There was a great, soft bed with a naked strumpet on it. Around that bed were six chairs."

"Yes?"

"William, they bade me fornicate with the whore or forfeit that dinner, that room, that bed, and suffer a flogging into the bargain."

"What? You call that punishment?"

"This is no joke, my friend. Almost every night for a year I dreaded the sound of the key turning in that lock. Sometimes the room would fill with strangers who had bought tickets at the gate. And I performed for them like a posture moll, nights beyond number. They saw my cold arts of love with every kind of drab this earth has mourned: maidens, hags, fatties, and greyhound-girls. I swived a world under those evil eyes.

"After a year of such abuse, I rebelled."

"Rebelled! Against what? Fresh sheets, warm blankets, good food, and more woman-flesh than any one man deserves. Pah! To think that Neville was arranging weekly prayer meetings on your behalf—and that I attended! Great are thy works, O Jehovah!" He shook clasped hands at St. Martin's steeple.

"William, you are my friend, and I know your jests to be insincere."

"Don't be so sure!"

"It's one thing to think a thing and quite another to perform it. It wasn't as you imagine it. There was a girl, a woman...her name was Jill..."

"And she won your heart, this Jill?"

"Who can say?"

"So she was special, then?" William gurned.

"Desist, Mr. Supple. Suffice to say that from our first forced intimacy we knew our intercourse was not intended for such exhibition. So I rebelled."

"And?"

I was thrown back to my first dungeon, back with the vicious morons and madmen. I was awarded one thousand and five hundred lashes to be administered over the remainder of my sentence. I should have died from the clap, I swear, but God—Neville's God—must have spared me and I left the Bridewell without a sore."

"And Jill. What of her?"

Buckram shrugged and shook his head.

"And now you're a struggling tractseller, in love with a woman of virtue, above your station."

"As you see me."

The Charioteer was as packed as ever. One o'clock was a busy time in Brydges Street. There was room to move, but only just.

Stepping back into his old haunt, William was consumed by a sense of despair; this was the world he'd left behind. This was somewhere he knew too well: the shallow, circular talk, full of lies, all the forced, dead-eyed bonhomie fueled by gin and the flower of the hemp seed, the over-embroidered coats, the sad, pompous lamb's-tail wigs, the shoeless, shuttling messenger boys—some old enough to be his father—waiting for an errand or some sinister, new friend to buy them drinks.

Bambara, Mandinka, Wolof, Fulani, Ibo, Whydah, Ashanti, Coromantee, Fanti, Ga, Hausa, Yoruba, Angola— William knew them all, even if they didn't know themselves. William was a Wolof. That's what Gullah had told him. Gullah was the only octogenarian slave William had met. He had been brought to the Americas as a twenty-year-old and had toiled on Blackstock's Plantation ever since anyone could remember. The old African used to wait for the young William when he had finished his chores. Together they would walk through the fields and along by the cabins. Gullah talked of a world so unlikely William took it to be imaginary. It was a black world of black kingdoms where black people did black things.

William was glad Gullah wasn't here with him in the Charioteer to see just how much cheap London gin could tame an Ashanti like Old Morris, or how extreme poverty and isolation had compelled an Angola woman like Molly to market her maidenhood.

The Charioteer was the safest place he knew for blacks in London and William hated it.

On seeing him enter, a number of St. Giles's Blackbirds saluted cautiously. He returned the gesture and let Buckram maneuver him through the press; he had nothing to say to them.

The two friends found space at the bar.

"Michael, scurvy grass are!" hollered Buckram.

They watched the quiet-looking barman fill two tankards with ale. He set the drinks before them and gave William a knowing wink. "You're a stranger to Brydges Street, aren't you?" he clucked.

William just laughed and mumbled something inaudible.

"You see how it is," said Buckram motioning to the room. William supressed a mild wave of nausea and turned to examine the boisterous clientele.

Old Morris was still doing the rounds with his glass of towrow, mocked and rebuffed by table after table. Quintus Greene, alone and smiling drunkenly by the empty hearth, sucked at a bottle. He used his waist to rock his wheeled trolley back and forth to music only he could hear.

Henry Prince was standing on a table teaching a group of white men with bandaged heads and split noses a new dance.

"Happy, though, aren't they?" Buckram added.

"Yes, desperately."

Two groups of drinkers exploded into a knife fight in the corner. William and Buckram turned their backs on the scene and looked into their foaming cups.

"What would you do?" asked William, "what would you do if all of a sudden you came into a couple of thousand pounds? Just like that. How would you spend it? Two thousand pounds."

Buckram stared at him like a condemned man. He took a sip of ale, dodged a flying bottle, and said, "Do you know, that's the second time someone's asked me that. Georgie put the same question to me not so long ago."

"Did he now? That makes two of us."

They laughed nervously and shook their heads.

The fight was rolling over to their part of the tavern, so they shouldered through the crush—ale held high above their hats—to stand by the door.

"He's up to something," said William.

"For sure."

"Something big. I can feel it. Has he spoken to you recently?"

An unwilling fighter was making for the exit. His enemies, or maybe his friends, grabbed him and threw him back into the fray.

"I haven't seen him in over a week. I'm avoiding him, truth to tell. I owe him money."

"Over a week. That's a long time for the George. He must be hiding out. Planning."

"Hmmm. Big plan. You interested?"

"Forget it. He's poison. You forget it too."

They heard the unmistakable cry of someone who has just been stabbed. The injured man swiveled frantically and a jet of blood arced from a throat wound.

William watched, fascinated, as alcohol attacked blood in his tankard, making it dissolve, turning the whole mess purple. Blood was on his clothes and blood was on Buckram.

When Offaly Michael ordered the dying man's cronies to carry him out to the street both gangs turned on him, his staff and everyone in sight.

Buckram half-drew his sword-pistol.

"Why bother," said William. "Let them kill themselves. Let's go to the Denmark. Have a coffee. Something civilized."

As they crossed the street, from the noisy house to the quieter one, Buckram passed him a blank scrap of paper and said, "Write out forty-three for me, William. Numbers and letters."

London, 23 June 1786

As always, the American War returned to Buckram in his sleep. This time he was back at Biggins Bridge, running away from the battlefield through the April drizzle.

Boys with melted faces screamed at him for help (in German) and he fled past them into the woods where the trees were hung with the mutilated bodies of Jäger Korps soldiers—some of them still alive and likewise calling on him for salvation.

He was not running alone. Charlotte was with him somehow, skirts flashing across the forest floor, keeping pace. Her hand in his. He knew they were running back toward the bridge where an ambush lay waiting, but they couldn't stop their flight. Their feet propelled them against their will to certain doom. Breaking cover of the trees they met volley after volley of rebel gunfire. The air around them soon turned to swirling clouds of sulfurous smoke. They stopped, but the firing continued. They were standing unhurt in the misty middle of nowhere with musket balls chopping up the air around them. Field guns fired from the hillsides and he held Charlotte's hand more tightly.

"You're safe now," he told himself. "Safe now."

The cannons boomed, one after another, till their noise became a pattern, a tune.

Bells were ringing and Neville was saying, "Give unto the Lord the glory due unto His name; worship the Lord in the beauty of holiness."

And Buckram was awake, with perfect knowledge of his situation.

It was like this every Sunday morning.

Neville would stand over him with a pitcher of cold water and a sliver of soap, waiting for him to rise and accompany him to church. And every Sunday he would comply ungrudgingly.

He didn't like church as a rule, especially a church like St. Giles where black people formed a sizable part of the congregation. It reminded him too much of his plantation life, when an overseer would ride down to the shacks on the Lord's day to read to kneeling slaves from the chapter in Ephesians where it beseeched obedience to "them that are your masters according to the flesh, with fear and trembling." Buckram hated hymns too. White people's hymns were so joyless; black people's hymns were just too inane.

Still, he'd had a bad week working for Henry Prince and Georgie. With only three copies sold in the last few days, he wasn't too proud to hope for divine intervention. Besides, the church was normally packed with all sorts of folk.

He folded up a copy of the *Secret Papers* and slipped it into his waistcoat.

One never knew.

Buckram was the last worshiper to arrive. He took a place in the back pew beside a beaming usurer and his family.

Neville was busy, in his element, padding down the aisle, handing out cushions and hymnals with flamboyant grace.

The church was a beautiful building, supported on the inside by Ionic columns of Bath stone. Stained glass in the east window depicted Abraham offering Isaac as a sacrifice and the angel restraining him. Light poured through this delicately wrought scene onto a massive organ in the west gallery. The altar piece had a scrolled pediment supporting a golden eagle in the middle and, above it, the head of John Smyth, the vicar, could just be discerned. The preacher's voice snaked out above the congregation.

Buckram tried to follow the sermon: "...according to Habakkuk, chapter 2, verse 2, 'For the vision is yet for an appointed time...'"

Zealots scuffled pages in their bibles, racing each other to the quote. "'...but at the end it shall speak and not lie: though it tarry, wait for it; because it will surely come, it will not tarry.'"

Nursemaids in the middle seats silenced babies and scolded toddlers.

He moved drowsily through the motions; picking up a prayerbook, opening it at random, and rising to mouth hymns.

Six rows in front of him, across the aisle, he noticed a young, pert, weasel-faced black woman. She was sharing a prayerbook with Charlotte Tell.

Immediately he was aware of his clothing: his shirt was clean (he washed it daily), but the waistcoat, breeches, and stockings were the ones she had seen him in three days before, and they smelled of Neville's sleeping quarters.

He left the church before the collection plate reached him and walked about the churchyard, rehearsing his introduction, till the service was over.

Beyond the low stone wall St. Giles's High Street was unusually quiet. Sundays were the only time when birdsong could be heard in this neighborhood and he listened, contrasting the sweet chirpings with the sad music droning from the House of God.

As the congregation exited he positioned himself by the gravestones, pretending to be lost in their strange inscriptions.

A tap at his shoulder. "Well, we meet again, Mr. Buckram." He swiveled round stiffly, smiled, and tipped his hat to Charlotte.

"So, you're a churchgoer, I see." She cocked her hatted head. "Have you met Mrs. Brookes?"

Her companion looked up at him, shielding her eyes with a fan. She curtsied and said, "You're a writer, I understand?"

She had spoken about him.

"You may know my husband, Mr. Aaron Brookes, the navy cook. He's a compatriot of yours. We have lodgings in Bainbridge Street, round the corner from here."

Buckram knew the street but not the family. So many blacks and ex-slaves from the Americas lived in St. Giles.

"I thought your church would be St. Paul's in the Piazza," he said to Charlotte, at a loss for anything more substantial to mention.

"By rights it is, but I do find the ambience there so...so...white."

He rubbed his right ear, wondering what she meant by

that. Black people don't always make a black church.

"It is my habit, after Sunday prayer, to take an Indian luncheon at the Lascar House in Newport Market. Would you do us the honor of accompanying us, Mr. Buckram?"

Buckram smoothed his empty pockets and noticed Neville lurking behind the church doors, watching them earnestly over an armful of prayerbooks.

"Alas, I must disappoint you, ma'am. I have an appointment with the verger of this parish, a Mr. Neville Franklin of Virginia." This was the saddest lie he'd ever told; all the sadder for the mounting pride felt in the telling.

"Oh, pity," said Charlotte, scrutinizing his clothes. "Never mind, perhaps you will be able to visit me in person this evening at my home, seeing as you've been unable to send over your friend's work."

"I've been busy," mumbled Buckram.

"Too busy even to send someone?" Charlotte pointed to a man crouched by the church gates with a sign round his neck reading "Messages delivered and errands run."

"You live at number forty-three, Long Acre, beside the sodmitical tavern?"

She laughed, k-k-k. "You have a good memory. You won't forget to call, will you? Tonight will be a very important night." She grabbed his wrist. "There's such great news. So much to celebrate."

He felt her hand grip, release, and grip again.

"And at what time will you be expecting me, Miss Tell?" he asked, carefully modulating the pitch of his voice.

"Oh, anytime around seven o'clock. I'll be waiting."

She laughed again and sauntered off arm in arm with Mrs. Brookes.

Buckram watched them till they vanished into Denmark Street. Neville and the Reverend Smyth were heading off tonight for a week-long tour of the shires to lecture on the evils of slavery. He rubbed his hands and clicked his heels before turning back to the gravestones to search for fresh flowers.

London, 23 June 1786

William counted his money...one hundred and forty...one hundred and fifty...one hundred and sixty...till he'd fanned out two hundred and seventy-five pounds on the bedspread before him. It was enough to pay the passage of his wife and sons over to London, but it wouldn't be anywhere near sufficient to keep them in the style to which he'd become accustomed. Looked at squarely, it wasn't much to show for two years' living in the imperial capital. How could he explain the sources of his income to Mary? Mary, who wouldn't even dance on the Lord's day—Mary who wouldn't even dance.

He tried to imagine everyone (himself, Mary, Phillip, and Nehemiah) living together in this room here on Rose Street. The picture was all too clear and he winced at it: Mary sniffing at the activities in the cockpit and sneering at the unwashed Covent Garden drabs with whom she'd have to share a communal kitchen; Nehemiah rifling willy-nilly through his collection of first editions and fighting with Phillip over who would sleep in which corner, who would fetch water from the pump, and who would wash first. The children with their dark faces and plantation manners would have to be weaned away from the market ruffians seeking to befriend them. He saw his new weekends: stagnant Saturday evenings spent reading edifying texts in the huddled bosom of his family, the interminable afternoons passed in the Pleasure Gardens of Ranelagh or Vauxhall. On Sundays, he knew, Mary would troop them off to worship at the Piazza church—a family treat. And schools, new clothes, new shoes, the sheer daily bread...where'd he find the money?

He asked himself again, as he asked himself time after time, What am I doing here? The answer came as it had come time after time: he was a free man. In London he was free to rise and sleep when he chose, free to read whatever he chose, and free to correspond with any like and literate mind. William fingered the spines on his bookshelf and reflected glumly on his copies of *Gentleman's Magazine* (to which he'd stopped subscribing a month ago after a virulent series of editorials attacking the black poor). Over the years his letters from Mary had grown fewer and farther between. The family was back in Carolina, he believed, but where he no longer knew. He hadn't received a letter in over four months. He was worried.

He shuffled his wad of money together and replaced it under a loose floorboard. He picked up George's sparkly gift from the bedside table and opened the lid. He let the nursery rhyme play as he considered the possibility of Mary's ever hearing it.

It was late in the evening and his muddled thoughts and the gloom in the room were getting to him. With a decisive grunt, he snatched a frock coat from the wardrobe and marched out the door.

Thinking of Mary always drove him to spend. He knew what he was doing and he didn't like it. He was buying time, buying peace of mind.

He traipsed toward Leicester Fields with a heavy heart, feeling the rough-grit roads under his new shoes and sensing the wear on his two-day-old heels. If he won enough tonight he could buy another pair of boots and leave his second set in Buckram's keeping. Old Uncle Buckram, pimp and love-struck fool, and Mad Old Uncle Neville, still doing the Lord's work in his threadbare uniform. Phillip and Nehemiah deserved better than this, and he, William Supple, would make sure they got it.

He stepped up his pace as he approached Hog Lane. Some Conduit Court cutthroats had established a new outpost at the corner of St. Martin's Lane where anybody who looked as if they didn't belong to the locale could bank on being shillied. Their presence didn't bother William. He passed that way daily, and besides, he knew how white people thought. They'd see a dignified black man wearing new boots, new stockings, and a clean blue coat of the kind they could never afford, and they would take him for a boxer or a Blackbird—a violent, well-connected man. Not to be messed with. He knew they would think twice. He trotted past with firm deliberation. He heard nary a grumble but he felt the ruffians' eyes on him, tracking his course into the side streets leading to Leicester Fields.

The square had been redecorated since his last visit. Chinese lanterns were strung out along the handsome facades of the freshly painted buildings. Crowds of prospective gamblers, strumpets, and their culls promenaded through the over ordered gardens in the cool evening air. As usual, the place was full of twittering couples. William found himself walking behind a well-dressed pair heading toward the Picadilly end: a black man and a black woman walking hand in hand. He was stunned to realize that he'd been following them from Hog Lane, transfixed by this most unusual sight in a city full of wonders.

Hoping to overhear a familiar accent, he moved closer to them. But they were clearly lovers, or a bored, overfamiliar couple whispering one to the other the strangled language of their desire.

He wondered where they'd come from, where they lived. What wayward impulse to happiness had driven them to stroll with such calm confidence here in the heart of the white man's world? It could be Mary and himself three months hence. Or maybe not. He remembered. This was a Sunday. This would never be. Mary, the real Mary, came back to him anew: her hesitant speech, her stalled laughter, her terse, critical asides, her haughty Baptist demeanor, her astringent body odor, and the touch of her skin, so different, yet so similar to that of the women he'd known in this town. He cursed his inability to remember her face clearly. And looking back at the black couple, now turning around and retracing their steps back to Hog Lane, he knew he'd never be that man, Mary'd never be that woman. Mary's heart, he felt, was still set on their original goal of Nova Scotia. She'd quickly wither and perish in this rough-and-tumble world he'd come to love. Maybe she was right. The Canadian blacks seemed to have more going for them. They had their own towns, their own churches, they farmed their own land, and knew white people only as distant neighbors or yearly tax collectors. He ambled through the square and tried to compose a new missive to his beloved.

"William!"

He almost jumped, but he didn't break his stride. He'd been speaking to himself a lot these days. Self-address was normal. "William Supple!" The voice was accented, insistent, not his own. A figure drew up alongside him. It was one of the triplets in civilian clothes. His young face glowed with excitement.

"William, look at you! On your own on a weekend, dressed in your finest. Let me guess. You're going to gamble?"

William nodded and laughed.

"Then you must be desperate." The triplet patted him on the back and looked him up and down.

"Which club are you headed for?"

William scanned the public houses and gaming rooms encircling them. Everywhere was full tonight. He had money to make. He wasn't sure if he wanted company.

When was the last time he wanted company?

"I'm uncertain what the night will hold," said William. His side tweaked as if in anticipation of further disruption. "I didn't get the chance to thank you and your brothers properly for saving my life that time."

"Oh, that was nothing." The young man bowed his head bashfully. "You'd do the same if it was the other way around. Wouldn't you?"

Knitting his brow, William said yes.

"We didn't see you at the rout. Thought you'd have pitched up with your buckos. Anyway next time, yes?"

William was about to reply when the triplet grabbed him by the sleeve and dragged him gently to the west side of the square.

"Where are we going?" William inquired lazily. Black men behaving bizarrely no longer disconcerted him.

"I'm meeting a friend at the plum-pudding stall. A great fellow. Knows all the kens. He's from the colonies, like yourself. You should meet him."

William let himself be tugged off course, painfully aware that the young guardsman was taking pity on him.

Three black men were gathered around the pudding-seller's cart. William recognized the two other triplets who, like his guide, were in civilian dress. The third man, frock-coated, unwigged and unhatted, was also familiar to him.

"Hail, Georgie!"

"Hail, Willie-boy! What brings you here? You know these soldier boys?"

William shook hands with the other brothers, for once relieved to be among people he knew.

"Of course I know them. It's a long story. Well, friends, what news?"

"The regiment is shipping out to Martinique in a few months' time. We won't be with them tho'. Killing black men for white men, forget it! We've other plans, other ideas, eh, George?"

Georgie said hmmm and stroked his cheek. "Good to know you've still got friends, Will. Tea? Pudding?"

They hovered for a while between food and drink stalls. The guardsmen paused to laugh at a pair of white buskers bashing tambourines. They tipped their hats at any young woman who crossed their path. Every half minute or so, passers-by shouted greetings at Georgie. Georgie told the triplets tales of his and William's scrapes with the Charlies back in the old days and of their tall-story sessions at the

Golden Cross. Being the object of the Beggar King's gentle joshing was not unpleasant and William felt something akin to tenderness meshing beneath the man's ribaldry. But he'd known Georgie too long and accepted that emotional intensity, not constancy, was the scoundrel's stock in trade. So he wasn't in any way surprised when Georgie clapped his hands and declared, "Well, Willie, you have yourself a nice evening now. Me and the boys have some business to discuss over at the Assembly House up Kentish Town way. Might tell you more about that some other time. Down at the Charioteer one night, yes?"

"Sure," said William. He watched the foursome leave the square, hot on the trail of two young dairymaids.

His urge to gamble had evaporated and his solitude soured to loneliness. He set off back to Rose Street; he had a letter to write.

Hog Lane was unusually empty for this time of night. All the pedestrians seemed to be streaming toward St. Martin's. William followed them to the junction and saw that the road had been cordoned off. Charlies were policing the crowd, so he positioned himself against a wall at the rear of the congregation, hoping to make himself less conspicuous.

Fire trucks were clattering up St. Martin's Lane from the Hand-in-Hand fire insurance office in King's Mews. As the cordon was lifted the crowd, now fifty strong and infected with the lure of disaster, chased behind the firedrakes. William raced along with them. He sprinted to the front of the pack and made it onto Long Acre just before a new cordon was strung across the street.

Heavy, acrid smoke rose from the backstreets and mantled the rooftops of Covent Garden. Weeping women in blackened clothes were being comforted by those who had made it past the cordon. A bruised and coughing young girl staggered out from Conduit Court and hurled herself into the arms of the first male figure she saw. William Supple.

The gambler held the sobbing child and brushed dust and cinders from her hair. Her face and shift were burnt in places and when she coughed he caught a dense whiff of smoke. She shivered.

"There, there," he said, comforting her, "you're safe now. No need to cry."

She rubbed a sleeve into her face, smearing soot everywhere.

The hiss and crack of flames eating old timber sounded dangerously close.

"Where's your mummy and daddy, littl'un?" asked William affecting London English.

"I don't know," she howled. "I don't know! Our house was burnt down with all the others." She began to cry again.

"Now, now," said William. "That won't do, will it? What we'll do is get you a nice, hot dish of licorice tea with lots of lovely sugar, then we'll go find your parents. So tell me, where do they live?"

She sobbed herself quiet and replied, "Rose Street."

"Wha' the…!" William flung the distraught child away from him. He ignored her screams as he dashed with all speed through Conduit Court and along Hart Street to the glowing mouth of Rose Street where the fire crews had assembled their carts. Firemen, wearing only leather gloves and casques for protection, leveled hoses at the blazing buildings and waited for their colleagues to re-commence work at the hand pumps. William edged round the fire-fighters and looked into the alley. One whole side of Rose Street—his whole side—was afire. Flames wrapped the walls of the Coopers' Arms and lapped across the frames of neighboring houses. Grappling hooks had been thrown up to catch on rafters and sills and gangs of firedrakes strained at the ropes, trying to pull the structure to the ground. William heard the mournful, suffocated bellowing of some doomed souls still trapped in the cockpit, baking alive in a subterranean inferno.

A short, sweating fireman carrying a small keg jogged past William. The firefighter stopped in his tracks and turned back to ascertain that a black man was actually standing there amid the conflagration.

"Oi, off! You can't stand there, you great, black ninny-hammer. There's a fackin' fire goin' on 'ere."

"That's my house!" William squealed.

"Your 'ouse?" The fireman looked at him, disbelieving. "Well, it 'int your'n no more, I'll tell you that. This'll see to it." He tapped his little keg. "Don't want the whole parish on fire, do we? You just stay out of our way 'n' watch the fireworks. Heh-heh-heh!" He ran toward his mates shouting, "All away, lads, all away!"

Hoses were reeled in and grappling hooks stowed away. The last of the firemen came away from the ruins and stood, with the transports, far round the corner in Hart Street.

The keg carrier unplugged his barrel and, walking backward, proceeded to pour a trail of gunpowder back along to Rose Street. He zipped back to join his mates and with great enthusiasm touched a lighted match to the trail.

William watched aghast as the fizzing white light sped around the corner.

He had heard louder explosions on the battlefield, but he had never felt one like this. His ears popped as the explosion boomed into Rose Street, then reverberated through the adjoining labyrinth of courts and back-doubles. The very ground shook three or four streets away from the epicenter. The blast deafened him and he couldn't hear the firemen crowing by his side. He tried to scream but found himself breathless. The explosion was drawing all the air from the surrounding streets into itself. Soon, an almighty crump signaled the final collapse of the Coopers' Arms.

William walked away, rubbing perspiration from his face and neck. So, he had lost his home and his possessions. God knew how many wretches now lay entombed beneath the place where once he'd lain his head. He was homeless and penniless. He straightened his shoulders and shrugged. It wasn't the end of the world. He had bounced back from greater misfortune than this.

He stalked off down Long Acre, registering the stark facts of his condition—all the more stark for the absence of any corresponding emotions.

So, he was a sadblack again with nowhere to hide save the sleek clothes he stood in. Everything was gone again: his wardrobe, his furniture, his bed, and, most of all, his money, his books, the magazines, and the letters. It was the sanctuary of paper that he'd miss most. Paper, he realized, was the one thing that kept him in touch with human life. Without it he was nothing, simply spinning idiotic fictions in voids of his own creation; like Buckram, illiterate, insolvent, invalid.

As he tramped past the Wheatsheaf public house he noted, by its side, a door daubed with the number 43. He looked at the open windows two stories above him and heard a strange, yet undeniably black female laugh, high and mocking: k-k-k-k-k-k. Buckram would be up there now, he knew. But this was altogether the wrong time to be knocking on strange doors requesting favors.

His steps took him instead round the corner into James Street. He cut through the marketplace, brushed aside the more insistent doxies and made his way along Russell Street, down Drury Lane, and into Brydges Street. The Charioteer was always open.

For William Supple it would be open for quite some time to come.

London, 23 June 1786

It was a bigger house than Buckram had expected and when he knocked on the door a gaunt white man answered.

"Aye?" He was a Lowland Scot.

Buckram knew he wasn't mistaken, this was definitely number forty-three.

"I've come to visit a Miss Charlotte Tell, the school-marm."

"Mr. Buckram, I presume?"

Buckram said yes.

"Above," said the Scotsman, ushering him in. "Follow me."

Buckram walked behind him up a flight of stairs, feeling foolish with his bunch of wilting tulips.

Charlotte was laying out fancy cutlery at a table set for five. Behind her on a chaise lounge two earnest-looking black men were locked in animated argument. On seeing Buckram enter the room they rose to greet him as if he were a woman.

"You're just in time, Mr. Buckram," said Charlotte. "Do come in and make yourself at home."

Buckram wondered what was going on. A smell of stewing chicken filled the apartment.

"Mr. Thomas Hardy you've already met," she said.

The Lowlander said, "Aye," closed the door, and brushed past Buckram to stand beside her other two guests.

"Allow me to present Mr. Olaudah Equiano, though you may know him better by his nom de plume, Gustavus Vassa of the *Public Advertiser.*"

Buckram didn't know him. Olaudah had an extraordinarily serious face. His eyes brimmed with awesome sanity. It was the sort of face to which only outright victories could bring a smile.

The third man, Mr. Ottobah Cugoano of the Gold Coast, resembled William Supple with his look of a well-flogged ex-slave, old before his time.

"Tulips, how sweet!" Charlotte took the flowers and carried them into the kitchen.

Two empty wine bottles stood on the varnished floorboards beside the chaise lounge. Ottobah opened a third and poured for himself, Buckram, and Thomas.

The men found seats and studied each other for a while longer than was comfortable.

"Charlotte informs me that you are a man of letters," Ottobah ventured.

"I live in the world of words, it is true," replied Buckram, surprising himself by the ease with which he spoke.

"Perhaps then you can settle an argument we were enjoying prior to your arrival."

"Speak on, sir."

"My good friends, Tom and Ola here, maintain that the work of old man Sancho is superior to that of Gronniosaw. For my part I disagree, finding Sancho's prose as stale and unappetizing as the almond custards his wife sells in that dreadful shop of hers. What do you think?"

"Firstly," said Buckram, "like all of us, I am acquainted with the Sancho establishment and do not wish to speak ill of the dead. In his defence, however, it must be stated that his widow is a purveyor of the most exceptional apple dumplings."

There was a pause, then everyone, except for Olaudah, exploded with laughter.

"Capital, sir! Capital!" guffawed Thomas. "But seriously, as a writer yourself, which do you find the more meritable document, Gronniosaw's *Narrative* or Sancho's *Letters?*"

Charlotte returned from the kitchen carrying the half-dead flowers in a china vase. She placed it at the center of the table.

Buckram stalled, noticing Charlotte's eyes on him and feeling Olaudah's breathing from the other side of the room.

"I see no great difference between the two," he said. "I find them somewhat alike."

"As chalk and cheese?" inquired the Lowlander.

"Surely, Mr. Hardy," Charlotte interjected, "surely you mean as charcoal and chocolate."

"Of course, ma'am. Of course. My mistake." He chuckled.

Buckram had never seen a white man behave like this in black company. He had never met a woman like Charlotte who felt free enough to invite four men to supper. And just how well did she know these three anyway?

They dined on ground rice and chicken cayenne.

"This is the dish available to our people in the colonies on feast days," Charlotte lectured Thomas. "I prepare it every Sunday evening as a sort of...a sort of sacrament, I feel. Strange as it may seem, it is very much the practice amongst many of us who live in these islands."

Some pains were being taken to overlook the Scot's strangled coughing and the beads of perspiration speckling his forehead.

Buckram sucked at the juicy, overpeppered chicken, envying Charlotte for never having gnawed the tough, meager sinews of plantation fowl, and wondering at her perfect skin, as yet untraumatized by whips and branding irons.

He wondered what it would be like to eat two large spicy meals every Sunday and how life would be if he could ever afford furnished accommodation.

Buckram emptied his plate long before anyone else. He settled back in his seat, to crunch chicken bones and marvel at the heady flow of intimate, cultured conversation.

"But it's all happened before, I tell you," Olaudah was saying. "Our brothers and sisters have survived such attacks and accusations many times in this country, most notably under Elizabeth, Good Queen Bess. She issued, again for reasons of political expediency, a proclamation ordering us to be discharged from her dominions, seeing how we supposedly relied over-much on 'relief' at the 'great annoyance of her own liege people.' This two hundred years ago, mark you, and yet, in spite of it and all of its kind, here we remain. More numerous than ever, better organized, an established community, I say."

"I'truth, Olu," scoffed Ottobah, "I suspect you romanticize our plight. We have, as you say, always been here, and I fear we always will. But only as hewers of wood, drawers of water, and sexual curios. More than that the English cannot abide."

"You do me wrong, Otto. I would not seek to undermine the gravity of our situation; I sought only to state that our numbers here increase and that we will become, if indeed we are not already, an ineradicable element of this nation's character."

"So, they frequent our clubs, sing our songs, dance our dances, and eat our foods. They do all that in the Caribbean and still flog us to death on a whim. Dammit, Ola, there are no ineradicable elements to these people; they're a composite of those they've conquered, and nothing more. Mongrels all, is that not so, Thomas? Is it not the same story in your land?"

"Aye, I regret to say that it is." The Scot whipped out a handkerchief and dabbed at his upper lip.

Olaudah stood up, glass of water in hand.

"A toast, ma'am, sirs, to our most honored guest and friend..."

Buckram stirred uneasily.

"...Mr. Ottobah Cugoano and, if he will permit, a toast in kind to his absent friend, Mr. William Green, on the successful release from captivity of our brother, Henry Demane, now safely resident on British soil."

Buckram imitated Charlotte and Thomas's polite cheering at this news.

Charlotte passed him a bottle of wine and a corkscrew. Olaudah and Ottobah noticed his awkwardness. He turned the items over in his hands until he divined their relationship and functions.

Charlotte made an excuse and left the room. The tenor of the mood plunged swiftly to the depths of acknowledged yet unspoken contempt.

Buckram struggled with the bottle, making off-centered stabs at the cork, trying to recall how Ottobah had accomplished the feat.

From the other side of the wall they heard Charlotte using a chamber pot. Her piss rang tinny and splashed deep, betraying the height of its trajectory.

Thick wisps of smoke from a nearby source floated through the half-open windows. Raised voices, bells, and frantic footfalls echoed from the thoroughfare below.

"Miss Tell tells us that you are promoting the work of an associate, Mr. Buckram," boomed Olaudah. "What is his name?"

"I fear I'd not be much of a friend if I revealed his identity."

"What! So you are sworn to secrecy? Name the fellow. Name his work."

"That I cannot do, sir. I am pledged."

Buckram had succeeded in penetrating the cork and was on the point of extracting it when Charlotte returned from the bedroom (with unusual haste for a young black woman, he noted).

"We were just inviting our brother Buckram to elucidate on his artistic endeavors. Are you by chance familiar with any of his writings, dear Charlotte?"

She shook her head and made too much fuss of clearing the table. She stuck her head out of the window and assessed the activity below. "There's a fire down the street!" she declared. "The firedrakes are out there. The road's blocked off. D'you think we're in danger here?"

"Heavens, no," said Olaudah. "They'll pull the building down, blow the damn thing up before the insurers will let the damage spread. Relax woman. Besides, you would, I am sure, be anxious to see something that Buckram here has produced, no?"

Thomas and Ottobah nodded with vigor. Charlotte compressed her lips and flashed Buckram a bewildered, pitying look.

Olaudah continued saying, "So, will you show us an example of your writing? What form does it take?"

"Poetry mostly," mustered Buckram, taking care not to make eye contact. He wrestled the remainder of the cork from the bottle neck and raised the bottle to his lips, no longer caring what impression he made.

"I suppose you'd like to hear some," he said without inflection. Somewhere, in the direction of St. Martin's Lane, an explosion tore through the night. Windowpanes, cutlery, and glassware rattled.

"A recitation!" Olaudah guffawed. "I'faith no, sir. We are all writers here. We must read for ourselves. Pass us the screed that we may examine it."

"The screed?"

Olaudah gestured disdainfully at Buckram's waistcoat. A single, folded copy of Henry Prince's tract poked out from the hem.

Buckram gasped. Olaudah snapped his fingers impatiently and stretched out his hand.

Still holding the wine bottle, Buckram stood up and moved to the door. "Charlotte, gentlemen, I fear I must disappoint you. The material I carry is unsuitable for general readership. It is of a highly personal nature, therefore..."

"Personal!" roared Olaudah. "Personal!"

"Ola, please," cooed Charlotte, "the neighbors!"

"I'll show you what 'personal' is!"

In one motion, he leaped up, leaned forward, and whipped the pamphlet from Buckram's waistcoat.

Buckram took a step forward to retrieve it, but Thomas and Ottobah were already on their feet and coming to stand beside their friend.

"Gentleman," said Charlotte shakily, "I beg you retake your seats. There is no need..."

Olaudah carefully unfolded the pamphlet, holding it some distance from himself. *"Aethiopian Secret Papers!"* he sneered. "I thought as much. You're nothing but a Piazza pimp, preying on the weakest daughters of Africa."

Buckram turned the handle and put one foot over the threshold.

"Miss Tell, gentlemen, if you'll allow me to explain..."

Charlotte came to his side, but it was only to open the door wider.

"I think you should leave now," she said.

He nodded, looking at the three men's expressions. Olaudah tore the *Aethiopian Secret Papers* into strips and, as Buckram plodded down the stairs, handfuls of it fell about his ears like confetti.

London, 28 June 1786

If only Buckram had a home to call his own...if only he could read and write...if only he had clean clothes...if only there was somewhere, anywhere, he could go without money...if only he'd not been born a slave...he could be smoking a pipe on the porch of some farmhouse out in Nova Scotia watching his crops blossoming under Canadian skies.

As it was, Buckram was sitting hunched over a cracked spittoon in Neville's shed. His stomach bubbled and rasped from three days without food, and his tongue could still discern strands of raw carrot wedged between his teeth from his last meal. He felt his bowels shiver as, once again, he buckled forward to spew out a thin stream of bittersweet bile. Exhausted, angry, and sad, he wished he could summon the power to leave his bed and even walk the short distance to Rose Street to visit William. He slumped back onto the thinning hay, cursing himself.

How could he have been such a fool? He was just another sadblack like all the rest, wasting away in sunless corners across the city, waiting to die. Maybe the army was the answer, or even a life at sea; at least he'd have regular meals, a place to sleep, and perhaps a chance to save a few pounds. But he couldn't live under orders from white men any more; he'd fought too hard and killed too many of them to return to such a life. Better to live under his own volition, even if that meant only another few days of hunger and madness.

Buckram lifted his head and scanned the darkness. There, against the wall, stood the old sword-pistol that he'd taken from the corpse of a fallen Tory at Blackstock's Plantation. William had taken good care of it; the scabbard was inlaid with tooled leather and mother-of-pearl, the blade itself was still sharp and well oiled. A handful of balls and caps were lying about somewhere. If it came to the worst he could always get a good price for it. He propped himself up against the wall and started to rock as he lamented the possible loss of his only weapon and the fact that his comrades had abandoned him. He rested his head on his knees and let time pass him by.

"Hello?"

Buckram jerked up from his morbid reflections.

"Hello? Mr. Franklin?"

It was Charlotte.

Buckram saw the hem of her dress sweeping the ground in the light beneath the doorframe.

He held his breath, praying for her to go away, hoping that she wouldn't knock on the unlocked door and tap it open.

"Buckram, it's me, Charlotte." She tapped and the door swung open. She squinted, wrinkled her nostrils, and walked in.

"So, you've tracked me to my lair," croaked Buckram. "Make yourself at home."

She remained standing, staring at him and cradling a wicker basket too tightly.

"How are you?" Her voice was barely a whisper.

"As you see me," said Buckram.

"I thought something like this had happened, so I took the liberty of coming here unannounced. I've brought you some food. Here." She placed the basket on the floor.

"I'm not hungry."

"Indeed not, sir. You do starve. Do you have a plate?"

"Of course not."

"I thought as much." She unfolded a green-and-white checked cloth and spread it over the cleanest area. From the basket she produced two pears, a quartern loaf, six slices of ham, a chunk of Cheddar, and a small, stoppered bottle of Bedford ale. As she put each item on the cloth she looked up at him, smiling broadly like a conjuror. She took a penknife from her indispensable and sliced and fanned a pear, the cheese, and the bread, then stacked them, together with the ham, into a triple-decked sandwich.

"Ma'am, you're too kind." He ate slowly and with great care, suppressing the urge to bolt down the food—previous bouts of near starvation had taught him that.

"You shouldn't have come here," he said.

"But I had to. I had to see how you were."

"Even after the way I disgraced myself under your roof?"

She just sat there, perched on the edge of the cloth, stunned and tender, as if he were a talking cat.

A clatter of wheels and hooves rang out in the courtyard. Buckram dropped his sandwich and stood up, shaking with alarm.

"Neville," he breathed. "Neville's back! He can't find

you here. You'll have to go." He held a finger to his lips and looked into the courtyard through a tiny knot hole in the wall.

Pastor Neville was helping Reverend Smyth down from a trap and setting a bundle of bags and books onto the grass verge.

Buckram sighed and shook his head—clearly, there'd be no end to his humiliations. He watched Neville accompany the vicar into the church.

"Now," he said to Charlotte. "Hurry, collect your things and begone from here. This is his house."

"House? This?"

"Hurry, woman!"

Charlotte scooped the food up in the cloth and began cramming it into the basket. Buckram bent to help her, stuffing the last of the sandwich in his mouth and hiding the bottle of ale. He had one hand on the latch and the other at Charlotte's elbow when footsteps sounded in the courtyard. Neville, carrying his satchel and Bible, was approaching the shed.

Buckram saw the preacher stop, turn, and start as a familiar voice hailed him from the street.

"Stay where you are. You cannot enter here," Neville commanded. Even in the thick of battle, Buckram had never seen such a look on Neville's face. He was scared grim and held his Bible out before him like a talisman.

"You may not pass." His voice quaked. "This is sacred ground."

There was a soft, rich chuckle and Georgie George flung a leg over the wall and walked into sight. The sun was at its highest point and waves of heat pulsated from the grass, yet he was still wearing his frock coat.

"Pastor, everywhere is sacred ground, yet, behold, I travel free. God alone knows where you get your ideas from."

"God! What do you know of God?"

"Wrong question, Pastor. You should ask: what does God know of me?"

"I am not afraid of you."

"Then that is good. It makes everything so much easier."

"State your business, then leave this place."

Georgie folded his hands behind his back. "I come with a message for friend Buckram."

"He'll no longer go a-pimping, if that's what you seek."

Georgie tut-tutted loudly and beamed. "No, Neville, I come with an offer of honest work." Georgie turned to face the shed and looked squarely through the knot hole. Buckram cowered in horror. Georgie could see him behind the wooden wall as if it were a pane of glass. Feeling stupid he straightened himself and returned Georgie's gaze.

"Tell him that he is expected at Peacock's the Printers in Drury Lane. There he will collect a number of posters to be put about the walls of the city. You see, Neville, the black townsfolk are organizing a rout next month at the Bull Inn. All are invited. Please feel welcome."

Neville grunted.

"Tell friend Buckram that he will be paid three shillings a day for four days' labor."

"Is that all?" asked Neville.

"All for now," said Georgie. "But you and I, preacher, have another appointment, I fear, some time in the future. Good day to you." He cackled and turned to walk away.

"I'm not afraid of you, imposter," bellowed Neville. "I know who you are."

Buckram heard Georgie shout back, "Everybody knows me, fool. Everybody."

Neville scuttled back into the church, crossing himself.

"Who was that?" asked Charlotte. "Is he a friend of yours?"

"Never mind. You must leave before Neville comes back. Go now." He unlatched the door and shoved her out. "This way, round the back."

They slipped into the alley beside the stables. Buckram helped her brush straw and mites from her skirts. His hands patted about her lower body and came to rest on her hips. He pulled her to him gently. She rested her head against his chest as he stroked her back.

She moved to kiss him, but his breath was foul, so she touched both his cheeks with her lips.

"I know you for who you are," she said. "You're a Blackbird, a free spirit."

"I'm hardly that," Buckram railed, cloaking his growing frown with a smirk.

"And you love your people," she added.

"And your friends, Ottobah and Ola. They do not?"

Charlotte sighed. "Their concern for our people weighs on them as a daytime duty, but by night they choose to consort with white women. You'd never do that, would you?"

"Me. Never." Buckram felt his heart thrown, like a skipping stone, across the waters of untruth, onto the bright shores of redemption.

"You needn't stay here if you don't want to," she told him. "I've room aplenty where I live. You would be most welcome."

"Charlotte, don't pity me, I beg you."

"I only want you to be all right," she managed to say.

He muttered, "Thank you."

They stood swaying together, head to head, in the cool, rat-filled alley. Charlotte looked up at him and giggled, k-k-k, and Buckram felt happy that he was loved at last and sad for knowing why.

London, 25 July 1786

Once—it seemed like a lifetime ago—William had asked Georgie where he lived.

"Oh, nowhere. And everywhere," Georgie had replied.

In the past weeks William had come to discover some of the truth behind that answer.

Georgie had no permanent address; most nights he'd be off to a different location to stay with yet another of his ever-growing circle of friends, lovers, and acquaintances. Some nights he'd spend going from ken to ken, from skittle alley to brothel, carousing till dawn and studying evil with diverse criminals. Otherwise, he could be found just walking about the city, talking to the mendicants and homeless people who'd elected him their king.

With Georgie problems never boiled down to money. He seemed to know everybody and money simply didn't matter when you had his kind of credit. Many a time William saw him leave for an evening's debauchery without a farthing.

Too much had happened to William in too short a time. His life as a dandy had vanished in the ruins of the Coopers' Arms. William the gentleman-gambler was now William the scrounger: back in Brydges Street. It mortified him to acknowledge that if it hadn't been for Georgie's good name he, William Supple ("the Negro Tragedian"), would almost certainly be homeless, hungry, or dead, and that Georgie took no pains to disguise the satisfaction he enjoyed in his playing a father to him.

William's name had been added to Georgie's account at several establishments, including the Piazza Coffeehouse, Tom's Coffeehouse (which he avoided, not wanting to meet any old dicing acquaintances), the Coach and Horses in Charles Street, the Pineapple in New Road, the Turkish baths on the Piazza, and the laundress's on Tavistock Street.

He took his meals at the Charioteer, signing for them on Georgie's slate. Under a similar arrangement, he slept there too, above the bar in a cramped, airless space. And, of course, it was Georgie who was granting him free entry to this evening's hop at the Bull Inn.

It was only a matter of time, he knew, before Georgie would be calling the favors back in. William hoped he'd be back on his feet again and away from places like Drury Lane and St. Giles before his friend started relying on him as a lookout or a courier. Buckram was the man to advise him now, but he'd seen nothing of him since he'd made a couple with Charlotte Tell.

Not long after losing his home, William had visited Neville's shed in search of Buckram. Buckram was long gone. Neville told him the Devil had taken him to live with a woman. The preacher's eyes had been wild and William remembered the sense of loss he felt as he listened to him rave. Neville had crossed the final step between eccentricity and madness. It happened to all blacks in London after a while and William saw it as inevitable. Unlike Buckram,

Neville had no social urges to charm him back from lunacy. He was gone. Gone to a world where Georgie was the Devil incarnate and Charlotte Tell his succubus.

Nowadays he looked in on Neville whenever he was passing St. Giles's High Street. The preacher could always be found talking over the gravestones of the illustrious dead, addressing Andrew Marvell, Godfrey Kneller, and Oliver Plunket as if they were present as children.

"Keep away from Georgie," he warned. "Don't let him over your threshold, or he'll get you too. He will, y'know, he will!"

William lacked the resolve to tell him that he was in very deed a guest under George's roof, living wholly on the man's charity. His tirades against Charlotte ("that she-captain of Satan") were wearing out William's patience. He could see a time coming when he'd have to leave Neville to the ministrations of the Reverend Smyth.

William had started to wonder if Neville had ever had any other friends.

A single, smoky lantern shed garish light over the crowd jammed into Bull Inn Court. The narrow passage was crammed with black partygoers dressed in some of the finest clothes William had ever seen. The overflow spilled onto Maiden Lane where more arrivals congregated waiting for the crush to thin.

A gang of white apprentices—William recognized them from the coach builders in Langley Street—gathered outside the steps of the Cider Cellar and studied the hundred or so black people with respectful fascination.

William had never seen so many elegant black women in

one place. He wondered who they were, where they had come from.

A few of them were dressed identically, sweltering under puffed polonaise dresses and short petticoats decorated with furbelows exposing nicely turned ankles. They all wore dangerously unstable wigs and extreme hats crowned with pink, white, and gold feathers. Not a shred of calico in sight. When they spoke it was with affected Mayfair lilts and Court-End phrasing. Their male counterparts were equally unbelievable in their purple and yellow coats, nankeen breeches and short-top boots. William overheard a number of them speaking in French about a recent trip to Copenhagen and a disastrous weekend away at the country seat of some lecherous aristocrat.

Who were these people? It was as if the memory of slavery had passed them by. As if they'd never known bondage. They were as free as a freeborn black could be in this white world and William didn't like the look of them; the haughty way they dismissed the shabby black tramps weaving between them with their begging cups and their mocking appraisal of their fellow revelers. They were all strangers to him, strangers to the rookeries of Ratcliffe and Seven Dials, strangers to the auction blocks of Wapping and the press-gangs that haunted the all-hour kens. Beside them, William felt like a failed actor, a ruined gambler, an unrewarded soldier, an ex-slave, and a sadblack.

He pushed himself into the crowd clogging Bull Inn Court, desperate to find someone he knew.

The noise from the crowd didn't quite drown the noise from the alehouse. Bass-heavy music rattled the glass and timbers of the Bull Inn. And the waiting throng, though packed solid, somehow moved in time to the music.

William found that he'd been squeezed to the middle of the alley. Standing on tiptoe he could see Henry Prince and Jack the Jamaican taking money at the door and arguing loudly with just about everybody. William relaxed his muscles, took a deep breath, and began to ease his way toward the door. At times he was practically crawling over a swarm of wigs and shoulders, like a salmon swimming upstream. He received blows. He returned some. He lost his hat. He made it to the door.

"Some rout, eh?" said Henry, squinting down at him.

"Some rout," he replied, catching his breath.

"Georgie's waiting for you inside."

Henry Prince turned to one side and waved him through.

The Bull Inn was large and cavernous. Baleful half-lights cast flickering shadows from dancers on the cracked plasterwork. A roaring fire blazed in a gigantic hearth in the far wall. It was tended by three old white women in straw hats. They turned a goat carcass on a spit and poked idly at a number of camp ovens and digesters slowly blackening in the embers.

The music makers performed on a stage of tables in the center of the room. Newton, Charles, and Hercules were up there playing the French horn, contrabass, and janissary drum. Seeing Charles staring at him William waved back, but the musician didn't respond.

William gasped for air and loosened his neckerchief. His skeleton had become a sounding-box, throbbing with the deafening drumbeats.

He pressed himself against the nearest wall, taking in the scene, trying to look part of it.

"Hot in here, isn't it?" Georgie George shouted into his ear. He'd popped up at William's side as if he'd just emerged from the cellar on a dumbwaiter. He held a Turkish water pipe in his hands and was swaying to the music.

"Seems a grand rout, George. But it's too hot. Too many people."

"That's the way I like it," he laughed. "The way it should be. A black man's hop. Look, Willie-boy. See them?" The Beggar King pointed his pipe at a couple who were holding each other's hips, half-stepping from this side to that every other beat, their eyes half-closed and locked in love.

It was Buckram and Charlotte Tell.

"Give me that!" William swiped the pipe from Georgie.

"She dances well, doesn't she?" Georgie held a lighted taper to the pipe while his friend inhaled.

"For an English girl, I mean, heh-heh-heh-heh-heh-heh," he added sharply.

William was old enough to know how little a woman's dance had to do with her sexual enthusiasm, but still. Looking at Charlotte—along with every male in the room—he had to shake his head, admit he didn't know everything, and take another mouthful of smoke. She was phenomenally beautiful, and Buckram, with reason, looked like the happiest man alive.

Georgie put a hand on William's shoulder and retrieved his pipe. "There's a room upstairs. A private room. I want you and Buckie to meet me up there at two o'clock." He saw William's face drop.

"Close your glands, man. It's nothing to worry about. Just a little proposition. Some business between me and my brothers." He jerked his chin at the triplets on the stage.

"Get yourself some food and drink. Mingle. Enjoy your damn self."

Before William could reply Georgie was at the door helping Henry and Jack sift the newcomers.

So this was it, William thought. Here they were again, he and Buckram, entangled anew in Georgie's machinations. The music continued around him, but he'd lost the urge to dance. This wasn't an English party, and he knew it would be a long night.

He went to the hearth and helped himself to a plate of cow-heel stew from a digester. He stood eating and scanning the crowd. The Mayfair crew had made it through the door and were huzzahing and hurrahing as if they were at the races. This was all new to them and William shuddered to think of the reports they'd give their white friends when they returned to wherever they'd come from.

There were whites in the dance, of course—Georgie's mates, five or six of them, dancing with clenched fists and fixed smiles, all studiously ignoring their drunken sister up on the tables among the musicians.

Buckram and his belle were still dancing, and William couldn't help glancing at them from time to time. Their passion for each other induced echoes of the old loneliness he'd taken such pains to suppress. It was two years since he'd held Mary and his children, and even though she disapproved of dancing and carousing ("wicked meetings with fiddlers!"), he wished her here with him now. He still nursed the hope that she could grow to love London. Phillip and Nehemiah, he knew, would love it to death. And who knew? Over here, they could grow up to be posturing fops, accepted and adored by those they mimicked. But more likely, they would end up shuffling about Ivy Street the rest of their days, cadging pennies and sleeping on kitchen floors and outhouse roofs. He still had a letter to write.

He took solace in another helping of stew. The digester had cooked the bones perfectly; they melted in his mouth like cheese. He munched away, watching the dancers twirl and skip.

Slews of glamorous, hard-faced ladies of the night passed him by without a glance, but he was used to this—the disinterest was mutual. Enshrouded once more in his arrogant solitude, he waited for the music to end.

He was still dreaming of his family when Buckram and Charlotte approached. Their faces glistened with sweat, and damp patches spread through their clothes. They looked like mischievous youngsters caught playing in a pond.

The two men shook hands and exchanged nods.

"Charlotte, my love, this is my very good friend, Mr. William Supple, another old campaigner."

She half-curtsied, mockingly, beautifully. "William Supple, the actor?" Her eyes shone with astonishment.

"You know of him?" asked Buckram.

"Why, yes." She turned her back on her consort.

"A pleasure to make your acquaintance, Mr. Supple. I once saw you in the role of Oroonoko at the Theatre Royal. You were splendid. A great improvement on the performance of Roger de Villiers."

"Indeed, it was, if I say so myself. I believe it was the black paint on his skin that made his playing the poorer."

Buckram laughed along with them, nervous and uncomprehending.

"And have you graced the stage since, Mr. Supple?"

"I have not, ma'am. The performance you witnessed was my first and last in this city and that on account of Mr. de Villiers' inebriation."

Buckram tapped Charlotte's arm. "My dear, you're being summoned."

One of the chic, quality black girls was waving frantically at Charlotte from the bar across the room. Long-limbed and goose-necked, she towered over her companions. She wore false eyebrows made from mouseskin.

"Lizzie!" Charlotte squealed. She careered through the party to join the elegant ladies and their gentlemen and disappeared under a storm of kisses. She seemed perfectly at home beside them. They were her people.

"Friends of yours?" William inquired softly.

"Friends of Charlotte's," said Buckram apologetically.

"Strange folk. Where do they hail from?"

"They're mostly from the Gold Coast. Sent over here to study. Some of them are in business with their parents. They all come from wealthy families. Y'know, merchants."

"Oh. That's merchants as in traders, yes?"

"Who knows," Buckram fluffed. "They're just business people."

"Dealing in gold, pepper, ivory, fishing rights...black humans. Hmmm?"

Buckram raised his hands and sighed. He shot a fresh glance at Charlotte's glitzy, young gang. They were readers and writers all, smooth world dwellers and Anglicised voyeurs far removed from the pain that ate him daily—they were bourgeois.

William had nothing more to say on the subject.

"Sorry to hear about your place, Willie."

William shrugged. "Just a fire. It happens."

"So, where are you living now?"

"Brydges Street, the Charioteer. Thanks to Georgie."

"Oh, God, so you're back running with him, then?"

"No, no, nothing like that. How about you?"

"I pasted up posters for the rout. Nothing more. Not now."

"I take it he's spoken to you about the meeting upstairs?"

"He has."

"And what do you think?"

"It's the big one. The two-thousand-pound question. I can feel it coming. He wants to tie us in with him. He never gives up, the swine. You interested?"

"I don't know. Maybe. It depends. I've no money and nowhere to live. I owe the George favors aplenty, and two thousand is a lot of money. I could send for Mary and the boys. Buy a house. Some land. It would solve a lot of problems, y'know."

Buckram nodded gravely. "Well, you were always the lucky one. Who knows, you could be lucky again. I'll go hear what he has to say, though. He's no bore, old Georgie, I'll give him that. But me, I'm not up for any more of the bastard's games. I've heard that big key turn too many times. And we both know who'll be on the other side. The man is a king bilker, second to none." Buckram shook his head and exhaled. "Truth to tell, Willie, I'm just too old. Must have turned at least thirty years. I've got my own life to live now. I'm having to settle down."

William looked through the crowd to where Charlotte stood, entertaining her friends with a hand dance and a balancing trick with a bottle of port. He wondered what she and Buckram found to talk about. Then again, remembering her moves on the floor, maybe they didn't talk too much.

The triplets had been replaced on the stage by the lipless runaway boy who begged by the Nag's Head. He was playing a weirdly syncopated version of "London Bridge Is Falling Down" on a borrowed guitar.

"He's playing my tune," said William.

The crowd tolerated the act until they realized that he was reading the music from a sheet of paper between his feet, and he was forced to leave the platform under a hail of boos and kitchenware.

"Shame," said William. "I was enjoying that. Ah well, drinks time. I'll get them."

William leaned against a pillar at the far end of the bar and waited to be served. It was going to take some time. There were fewer people in this part of the room. It was almost quiet enough for conversation. Charlotte's friend Lizzie was in deep gossip on the other side of the pillar with the woman everyone called Mrs. Brookes—no one, however, had ever seen her husband. William pressed closer to the pillar, keen to monitor their small talk.

"But, Lizzie, what are you telling me?"

"It's true. She told me this morning."

"Well, is she sure?"

"As sure as you can ever be. It's been almost a month now and she saw Dr. Burke yesterday."

"That old angel-maker! I wouldn't trust him to slice my kedgeree."

"The poor girl's at her wit's end. Doesn't know how to break the news."

"The sooner the better, I should say. Not the sort of secret you can keep for too long. She'll have to tell him."

"She can't. She's too scared."

"Scared of what?"

"She thinks he'll leave her."

"Is that such a bad thing? They're hardly the ideal couple. If I was in her place I'd..."

A loud burp erupted at William's ear. It was the white villain known as Pete Fortune. He was a chubby man with pigeon looks and ways.

"Got a long face, Bill. What yer thinkin' on?"

"Oh, women. How much they talk, y'know."

Pete Fortune laughed. "Well, it's just another way of screaming, you might say. Only that way it lasts longer and you can share it. Sort o' makes sense when you think about it."

William stroked his chin.

"Nice to see you round the old boys, again. We had some times, eh? Down Drury-side, fleecing those frocks."

"Yes, we did," said William. "Have a drink."

"Thought you'd never ask. Fill o' Stepney if you don't mind, bruv'."

William returned from the bar with a drink for Buckram. He asked his friend how he was feeling.

"Never better, Willie-boy. Never better."

"Buckie, go visit Neville some time. Some time soon. He's in a bad way."

Buckram said he would.

Just before the clock struck two, William and Buckram,

much fortified by ale, joined the three Grenadier Guardsmen and trooped upstairs to meet with Georgie George.

The Beggar King ushered them into a musty room with boarded-up windows. On the floorboards were two thin mattresses, both covered with crumpled, graying sheets. Georgie squatted in a corner like a fallen gargoyle and watched them arrange themselves as best they could.

"Willie-boy, Buckie-lad," he opened. "You're probably wondering why I've brought you here."

"No," they chorused.

"Aaah, you know me too well." He laughed darkly. "All the same, let me just say that once again we are gathered, we three from old Amerikee, this time in the company of our African bretheren, to discuss our mutual futures. I ask you now, gentlemen, to cast aside all the reservations you hold about my character. All the rumors, half-truths, and hearsay. This is no occasion for idle suspicion. We have no time for rancor or distrust. Let us convene as brothers of one flesh as I invoke the spirit of our native generosity and ask that you harbor no doubts as to my intentions."

He stood up, warming to his theme, entranced by his own eloquence. He began to pace, his left hand on his hip, his right hand poised to embellish his delivery. Laughter resounded in the stairwell from the party below. Eager white male voices were leading the crowd through a round of English country songs.

"Hear that," said Georgie. "Two peoples, one tune. Believe me, we'll never know just how happy that white boy is right now. Listen to him. He's singing his heart out like one redeemed."

The tune changed to "Lillibullero." Handclaps and the janissary drum threw in fresh punctuation, rendering the souless chant exotic.

"Tell me, Buckie, when was the first time you heard that?"

"During the war. It was a Tory marching song."

"That's right, and now they've got us dancing to it. That's the way they like things. Their blood, our heartbeat, their heartbeat, our blood—it's all the same to them."

"Georgie," said Buckram, "we don't give a turd for your philosophies. Just tell us what you want us to do. What's your plan this time?"

"Hear me out, my friends, hear me out. We all know that our lives are worth nothing in this country. No matter how bad you think things have been before, I promise you it will be as paradise compared to what they are planning for us now.

"Every day we see our brothers dragged away and incarcerated. You've all seen the public notices. I tell you, the Sierra Leone scheme is no longer a laughing matter. They intend to sweep us from the streets. They wish us evil. Within a year there will be no more black faces in London, save a few slaves and doxies."

William guffawed.

"You laugh, Mr. Supple, but d'you really believe they'll stop at shipping out just the beggars and sadblacks? No, I have it on the best authority that comprehensive clearance is afoot. So, William, Buckram, unless you both wish to stay and fight for the right to remain where you're unwanted, I suggest you join forces with me and our African friends here and work with us to chart our own destinies."

"Mr. George," said Buckram, "the hour is late. I beg you, say your piece and be done."

"My piece, as you put it, is simple. Hercules, Newton and Charles are already aware of my plan and have pledged themselves to it. I invite you to do the same. I invite you, for the sum of two thousand pounds, to live out your dreams, but before, grant me just one day. Just one day is all I ask. The rest of your lives will be yours to do with as you please."

The men watched Georgie. He drew a letter from his frock-coat pocket and the room fell quiet. The Beggar King had their complete attention.

"I doubt whether any of you are familiar with the American States Minister to the Court of St. James, a certain Mr. John Adams." He paused and looked from face to face.

"Some months ago, it came to my notice that his residence in Grosvenor Square is visited regularly by a number of Virginia planters and their agents. Since the end of the war, the rebels have been seeking cheaper, non-British sources for their slaves. Their embassies in Paris and London are used as bases for this commerce. Hitherto, they've made new contracts with Dutch and Portuguese traders.

"But being Americans, they continue to seek newer and less costly markets. I have here a letter from Mr. Hayden Irving, who will be a guest of Minister Adams next month. He has consented to meet with an African delegation headed by a Chief Birempon Kwaku, Mansa of Obomi, in an attempt to secure trading rights in human cargoes from an area of the Niger Delta. Due to the nature of his business, Mr. Hayden will be traveling with a sum of approximately twelve thousand pounds in notes and gold coin. Needless to say, there is no such land as Obomi and no Chief Kwaku. So far, our imposture has been successful, confined as it is to mere correspondence.

"All that remains is for you two gentlemen to combine your powers with ours and plan your futures accordingly. Any questions?"

Georgie seemed to be enveloped in a soft, shimmering glow, as if all the light and air in the room had drawn around him. No one spoke. It was a silence born of humility. Silence born of purest envy.

"Dreams, dreams, and dreams," he continued. "Let me tell you about your dreams. Friend Buckram, you are a born horseman, you rode the Long Chase with Tarleton's Legion through the Carolinas. That was your happiest time, was it not? And what did you gain for your efforts but wounds and a whipping? For two thousand pounds, will you be our escort and ride with us but for one day?

"William Supple, you remember our old sessions at the Golden Cross where, for the price of a measure of ale, we'd play Princes of Araby for provincial fools? You have the soul of an actor, the royal role becomes you. For the price of two thousand pounds, will you be our king for a day?"

Buckram got to his feet and walked to the door.

"Don't even think about it, William. George, not this time, not me. It was a good speech, but not good enough. I've been here before, remember. I know what happens when your plans go awry. Someone always takes a fall, and it's never Georgie George. It won't be me either. The last time was the last time. Good night, sirs." He left, slamming the door behind him.

William suddenly looked small and terrified.

"Don't worry about Buckie, Will. He'll be back. Now, where were we? Any questions?"

"There'll be blood and rumbustion, won't there?" William asked timidly.

"That shouldn't be a problem," answered one of the triplets—William couldn't tell which. "There's only a couple of infantrymen who double as footmen and gardeners. Unreliable types, drunks mostly. Then there's a black butler, no problem there, we hope, and the Minister, his wife, and daughter. That only leaves the house girls. Again, no problem. Besides we'll be going in well-armed. So don't worry about it. We're men-at-arms. The King's own. The best. Easy in and easy out. See you in Nova Scotia."

"There's something you haven't told me, George. Where in the world would you go with two thousand pounds? As a black man, I mean?"

"For my part, William, I have chosen Brazil, the north-east coast. The perfect place. As of tomorrow, I'll be making arrangements to book a passage on the next packet brig out."

"Brazil! But that's the worst slave-state on God's earth!"

"Not where I'll be going. Anyway, it's a hot country and it'll give me the chance to get rid of this damn coat and finally feel some sun on my skin. You should come, too."

"It's not so easy for me Georgie. I'm a man with responsibilities."

"The same responsibilities you've had for the past two years. What can you do here that can't be better done in Brazil?"

"I don't know. I'll have to think on it. What happens if we get caught? I don't want to swing at Newgate."

"None of us will hang because we won't get caught. This is a crime that will never be reported. A black gang robs the American Embassy of its secret slave bounty. Who would dare tell of it? The good citizen Irving of Virginia? Minister Adams? He's an ambitious man. He'd never hold public office again if the tale were told. Besides, who'd believe it?"

"So, Mr. George, what role do you play in all this?"

"Me? I'm your interpreter, of course."

Georgie bowed before him. "Chief Kwaku, your people await your reply."

London, 28 July 1786

Buckram sat frowning at Charlotte's writing desk. In an effort to forget the spelling primer and the blank slate between his elbows, he stared wistfully out a nearby open window at a lone seagull describing graceful arcs in the hazy sky. After a while his eyes fell back to the symbols in the children's textbook. He located the letter and tried again, remembering Charlotte's lesson: *c* the right way over, *c* the wrong way. Clenching his teeth, he hissed the sound, then puckered his lips to blow through the *es.* The rest read itself and the three words now made sense: *soon, sooner, soonest.* He used both hands to arrange the chalk stick in his ostler's fingers, but the marks he made, all save the *es,* were mirror images of what was on the page. He placed the book facedown on the slate and looked back to the sky, seeing the bird speed back to sea.

Still in his nightshirt, he fretted round the woman's room. It smelled of mildew, bay rum, and lust-charged nights. It was already noon. A pile of coins on the dresser reminded him of his chores: Clare Market for firewood and mutton, the Piazza for potatoes and eggs, the brass tongs and shovel to be burnished, a carpet to sweep, a news-sheet to buy.

Midday voices hollered down Long Acre: draymen,

costermongers, nosegay girls, watersellers, balladsellers, footmen, hackney coachmen, baker's boys, clerks, and coopers—working people on a working day. Soon Buckram would be out among them; he knew he'd look like a servant running errands and not a man in love. As usual, she'd left out the wicker basket for him, and, as usual, he'd take the muslin sack.

Sometimes he'd meet her at the schoolhouse gates and escort her home. A new gang of cutpurses had taken control of Conduit Court and had started making forays into Little Hart Street and the area around the Adelphi School. For all Charlotte's sophistication, Buckram knew she was a country woman at heart. She often complained about the violence in the city and the amount of trouble she experienced going about her daily business. There was the time two months ago when she and Mrs. Brookes had been invited to a reception at the Moroccan Embassy. A mob of river workers laid siege to the building and they had been trapped there all night, silently loading pistols in the dark with the Ambassador's young family and waiting for daylight or a detachment of guards, whichever arrived sooner.

His clothes lay around the room and he set about collecting them, item by item. As he fished under the bed for his stockings his hand brushed a small linen bag. He pinched it and felt it was stuffed with fabric. Hooking the bag out into the light he loosened the dusty drawstring. A dense, metallic odor wafted out. There was a bag inside the bag, and inside that he found a bound wad of rectangular cloths, some red, some reddish-brown, some almost black, each one quite stiff from its stain. Charlotte had written dates and notes on them in black ink. Buckram recognized the year 1786 but that was all; he couldn't follow cursive.

He passed a broomstick under the bed and discovered five more bags. They all contained similarly treated material, some with dates going back to 1781. He rifled through the bags feeling like a demon counting sheaves of underworld currency. What sort of woman? he wondered. What sort of woman? He sniffed his fingers, and, just to make sure, he stuck out the very tip of his tongue…

As the key turned in the door his stomach turned too, as if he'd swallowed a live mouse.

Come murderer, come footpad, come cadger, come thief, but please, God, not my Charlotte, not now!

She let the door swing open and stood there looking in at Buckram in his night clothes, on all fours amid her secrets. Her eyes blazed fury, her head tipped and locked at the wrong angle. She looked like a madwoman. Wide, swaying, clumsy steps jerked her closer, and she raised her right hand above her head as if to call down fire from heaven.

"I…" he said. "I…."

He got up and straightened his nightshirt as if that would give him more authority. "What's to tell? I was searching for clothes. I looked under the bed. I thought you were at school, so I chose to peek."

She drew herself up before him. He heard a rush of air and half a shriek.

The left side of his face exploded. He saw stars. She closed in. He raised an arm to ward off the attack, but it was to no avail; within seconds her rapid, steady blows had numbed his forearm. He was losing control of his limb, and very soon she'd be coming under his guard to damage his face.

He edged slowly round her and walked backwards, luring her through the door, onto the landing. If she was going to get nasty he'd prefer she did it away from any kitchenware. He'd have to catch her wrist and pin her down. They lunged at each other simultaneously, but his heart wasn't in it. Hers was, and, as she pulled him forward by the shirt, she rammed her right knee into his diaphragm.

"Charlotte," he wheezed, clutching his belly, astonished by her violence. "What's wrong with you? Have you taken leave of your...?"

She slashed at him again. He dodged the blow with a weary, almost bored, flick of his head.

"How dare you!" she rasped. Properly harnessed, that voice could have cut through steel. "How dare you!"

"By God, woman, I was searching for my clothes. What care I for your blood]rags! What brings you back at this hour, anyway?"

As quickly as it had erupted, Charlotte's fury vanished and her features regained their original composition. She snatched the bag from the floor, tied the drawstring, and kicked it back under the bed. She went to look at her face.

"Today is a Monday, sir." She spoke into the mirror. "I take but one morning class. I believe you've forgotten this?"

He had.

"And besides," she continued, "I've planned a treat for this afternoon."

"A treat, huh?" She might as well have said a kitten-stamping, so dour was she.

"It's a surprise." She began to arrange her largest, whitest wig on her head. "A little excursion."

Buckram's spirits plummeted. Charlotte had taken to

organizing all their recreations without consulting him. Her idea of a good time always involved the company of her hideous friends. His opportunity to escape had passed him by. He should have stalked out of the house in the heat of the argument, when he had the chance. But now he was stuck with her folly for the rest of the day. Charlotte was full of surprises, and it was killing him.

"Come now, Buckie. Get your clothes on."

"Do we have to leave now?"

"Why, yes. Mrs. Brookes should be calling for us shortly. And there are people waiting for us by the river." She smiled a secret smile. "Some very special people."

He was sandwiched in a bouncing post chaise between Charlotte and the ever-present Mrs. Brookes. Buckram ignored the catcalls and oaths their presence elicited from the Westminster pedestrians and sat out the journey to the waterfront in rueful reflection. Very special people. He shuddered at the thought. It could mean one of many things. Was he doomed to spend the rest of his life enduring Charlotte's taste in people and places? It was as William had warned: she was not of their caste. She was happiest surrounded by the flotsam of the black beau monde, timidly proffering the lowest bids at Christie's Auction Rooms, singing aloud in the Opera House, or huddled with a knot of radicals in the drafty back room of some Fleet Street alehouse, firing up their seditious fantasies with genteel sips of bland liqueurs.

"Here we are. Thameside, my good friends!" bawled the cabbie. They alighted near the cathedral beside some stone steps that led to the river. Buckram paid the driver with the money Charlotte had forced on him before they left the house.

"Oh, look," trilled Mrs. Brookes. "There's that grouchy egg woman from Berwick Street Market. Remember her, Charlie?"

"Oh yes," Charlotte stated flatly.

Buckram stared at the harridan on the steps. She was selling rotten vegetables, bad eggs, and old bones at tuppence a bag. "All yer bad stuff, ladies'n'gents! All yer bad, ready for the river! Chuck it or shuck it! Two pennies a sack! Get all yer bad stuff here!"

Charlotte sighed, exasperated. "I suppose we should take some for the crossing. It is a custom, after all." She purchased a mixed bag of lamb's skulls and greening potatoes.

"You'll need 'em 'n' all out there, you lot," barked the muck vendor, making the sign of the cross.

"Dare say we will," retorted Mrs. Brookes. "Dare say we will."

The river was at low tide. Its brown water sparkled prettily where wavelets caught the sunlight. Buckram guided the two women past teams of novice pickpockets working the stairs.

Very special people. Buckram saw them now, an odd party of three women and two men gossiping on the riverbank by a small ferry. He kissed his teeth on noticing the tallest member of the group. It was Lizzie, Charlotte's noisiest and nosiest friend. She sweltered in a pink riding costume. Her companions were a pair of middle-aged couples dressed in clean, unfashionable styles, and one of the women was white. Not Charlotte's usual crowd at all.

"Hello!" screamed Charlotte. "Hello! Praise be, you've finally made it!" She hitched up her skirts and scampered over the wet sand, leaving Buckram and Mrs. Brookes behind her.

"What's all this now?" grumbled Buckram discomfited by his beloved's hysteria.

Mrs. Brookes flashed him a cruel grin. "*On verra,*" she sang.

They batted their way through the curtains of flies buzzing about the party. Like Charlotte, the others had bought bags of rubbish on their way down. Charlotte was wiping tears from her eyes and wallowing in the fussy embraces of the black couple. Dismissing Lizzie's chortled greeting, Buckram strode up to the cuddling threesome.

"Oh, Buckram," she said, catching his arm and dragging him to the center of attention. "Buckram, I'd like you to meet my parents."

His jaw dropped. Parents?

"Pleased to make your acquaintance, young man." The kind-faced, gray-whiskered man offered Buckram his hand.

Buckram was paralyzed. This was something he could never have imagined: seeing a black adult in the company of parents. It was as much as he could do to gasp and take the older man's hand.

"Charlotte's told us all about you."

"The pleasure's all mine," blurted Buckram. He wondered how any black man living in England could radiate such open warmth as Mr. Tell.

"And this is my lady wife, Anne."

"Ma'am." Buckram tipped his hat and bowed to the tiny

woman with tired features. She emitted a squeak and returned the bow with more of a wince than a smile. Her eyes were like Charlotte's, though harder and more contained. She was unable to cloud the caution and dismay swimming in them.

"Oh, do hurry up!" implored Lizzie. "The boatmen can't wait all day." She flashed the pilot and oarsmen a toothy, apologetic smile.

The ferry was called Wheeler's Right.

"Are we to embark, or no, father?" asked Charlotte, sounding just like a five-year-old.

"One moment, daughter." He was still beaming at Buckram. "Our introductions are unfinished. Mr. Buckram, allow me to introduce our dear friends and neighbors, the Barbers, Francis and Betsy. They traveled down with us from Lichfield."

"Ah-hah, so you're our Charlotte's intended, are ye?" asked Mr. Barber.

Buckram stuttered.

"I'm joshing you, lad. Take no notice. Francis Barber, you may've heard my name mentioned in these parts."

Buckram shook his head, wondering why this man had adopted the mannerisms of a country squire. He slapped Buckram on the shoulder and wrung his hand too fiercely, as if to hide some private disappointment.

The Barbers were a short, good looking couple in their late forties or early fifties. Mrs. Barber curtsied and grimaced sweetly. She had the face of a white woman who has lived for two years in the heart of the English countryside with her outspoken black husband of ten years—she looked absolutely terrified.

"Oi! You crossin', or whet?" growled an oarsman. His fellow rower was lying asleep under the seats.

"To the Pleasure Gardens, then, my good man," shouted Francis. "Let's to Vauxhall."

As the ferry wobbled in the water, Charlotte blurted, "This is making me seasick!" She meant it. "I've got to get off. Tell them to turn back!" Crouching on all fours, she felt her way to the side of the boat.

"Gentlemen, row on," ordered Francis. "Ladies, restrain your sister."

Lizzie and Mrs. Brookes immediately shifted apart to create a new place for Charlotte. They held her carefully, but warily.

The ferry pulled out, rocking sharply as the oars cut against the current.

"That's not like her at all," said Mr. Tell, watching his daughter gulp and convulse. "My girl has never been a soft one. I blame this bad air. How can a man live within it? Is this not an accursed city?"

His wife looked at him as if he were insane.

"London," boomed Francis—Buckram thought he'd been too quiet for too long, "London, Queen of cities, all. Best place for a young man, let me tell you." He stood upright in the boat and (to his wife's ill-concealed dismay) began to recite:

> *Assemblies, parks, coarse feasts in city halls,*
> *Lectures and trials, plays, committees, balls,*
> *Wells, Bedlams, executions, Smithfield scenes,*
> *And fortune-tellers' caves and lions'dens,*
> *Taverns, Exchanges, Bridewells, drawing rooms,*

Installments, pillories, coronations, tombs,
Tumblers and funerals, puppet shows, reviews,
Sales, races, rabbits, and (still stranger) pews.

There was tolerant applause. The boatmen cackled. Buckram had never heard anything like it. The only part of the verse he could relate to was "Bridewells." Now that Francis had their attention he began to bore them with accounts of his perambulations and excesses in the company of "The Good Doctor Johnson."

Buckram felt relaxed enough with Mr. Tell to pose a quiet question: how did he and Francis Barber come to be friends?

"Young man," he whispered, barely audible above the oar-teased water, "Lichfield's a small place. My wife apart, his is the only black face I see." He scratched his ear and hunched his shoulders. "Can't always choose your friends, eh?"

"Indeed not, Mr. Tell," concurred Buckram. "Indeed not." This was the first time he had ever unmockingly addressed another black man as Mister.

"Oh, oh," said Mr. Tell, pointing at Betsy with her head over the side by the prow. "Not another sick woman, I pray?"

"I doubt it," said Buckram, checking the horizon and the bag between his feet.

Betsy had obtained a clear view upstream. Buckram saw how her muscles locked as another ferry rounded the river by Lambeth Palace. This ferry was full of bare-chested men with their hats turned back to front.

"Oh, Jesus, what new torment?" whimpered Charlotte's

mother as the other ferry changed course to draw up along-side Wheeler's Right.

"This, good woman," Francis declared excitedly, "is your famous London river josh. Great sport wouldn't you say, pilot?"

The pilot was completely uninterested.

"Let the ark ruffians make the first move," Buckram said aloud, reluctantly acknowledging his role as the most able-bodied male passenger.

"Ahoy there," hailed a river ragamuffin. "You ugly black sons-of-bitches! Your mothers are all bawds and your women are tupptney sups!" Much laughter.

"Ah, well," Buckram sighed. "Let's get it over with." He stood up and cleared his throat. "Talk to me like that! You chicken-stinking, cockless white bastard! Go bend for Satan and sear your mouthpiece!" With the exception of Mrs. Tell, the passengers and crew of Wheeler's Right cheered loudly.

"Talk to me like that!" came the reply, "I'll run a rusty needle through my ol' mare's doo 'n' sew up yer fat black lips!"

Buckram cleared his throat again. Someone patted his back. "Allow me," said Francis, eager to join the exchange. "You lousy crew of gray-bellied rats! The only clap you've clapped is your mothers! Talk to me like th...!"

A soggy onion flew across the water and caught him square on the nose.

"Oooh, that's it!" squealed Lizzie, pulling up her bag of muck. "Here we go! Have at them!" She hurled two rotten eggs at the onion thrower. They missed him, but one splattered neatly against the opposing pilot's neck.

The air was soon thick with malodorous missiles flying

between boats. Charlotte discreetly emptied her stomach over the port side as the battle raged.

Mrs. Brookes screamed. A heavy, pungent projectile had exploded on her apron. "Dung!" she gasped. "They've got dung! That's not fair. They're using dung!"

Buckram was holding his last lamb's skull, and Betsy was taking aim with baby carrots. Lizzie chucked a handful of compacted maggots. More manure was coming on board. It wasn't looking good.

The pilot of Wheeler's Right tugged a sack from the stern and tipped out its contents. "Here, use this." Great chunks of coal littered the deck around him. "And look lively! Won't get your hands dirty, will it?"

They pounced on the new ammunition and commenced a judiciously aimed barrage against the dung wielders. Two of their crew fell immediately. The river rats had run out of things to throw. The volleys of coal grew heavier, became demented, in fact. Even Mrs. Tell was up and lobbing. Buckram heard her laugh, k-k-k-k-k-k...

The enemy pilot pulled down his breeches and mooned at the black people. He singled out Betsy for a final piece of abuse, "Aaah, you dirty sow, better you marry a pig than a monkey. May dogs defile your unborn litter! Bugger the lot o' you!"

Francis launched a last lump of coal, but it fell short and splashed dead in the wake of the departing ferry. "The swine," he fumed. "Listen to them!"

The scoundrels sang as they sculled out of reach:

The Blackies have taken my sweetheart away,
The Blackies have taken my sweetheart away,

The Blackies have taken my sweetheart away,
Turra-lie,
Turra-lee,
Turra-lay...O.

Visitors were arriving at the Pleasure Gardens in flotillas of small ferries and wherries. Bands of mudlarks, equipped with brushes, waited on the steps to clean up the new arrivals.

Francis elected himself guide, but before they entered the park he insisted on having his shoes cleaned and he insisted that Betsy should watch him. While the bootblack set to work with his slop of egg white and lamp soot, the rest of the party dawdled at a liquor parlor decorated like a Moorish harem.

Buckram settled Charlotte on a bench beside a table lined with vases of tulips and minute glasses of syrupy beverages. He plucked a flower and rubbed it softly under her nostrils.

"For all that we have and for all that's to come," he uttered. He kissed the flower and placed it in her bag.

"Thank you. It's lovely," she said absently. She was staring at a doxy and her cull on a giant silk cushion.

Buckram drew up a stool and straddled it. "How d'you feel?" Charlotte's face had that deathly pallor unique to beautiful, ailing women.

"I'm fine. It's nothing. Nothing grave." She nudged Buckram's elbow, prompting him toward her beckoning father.

"What do you drink, young man?" Mr. Tell passed a hand over the table. "There's arrack, punch, ratafia, orange brandy. What do you want?"

Four jars of scurvy grass, thought Buckram. He settled for orange brandy. It was the smallest serving of the brightest color.

"You must let Charlotte bring you up to Lichfield one day," announced Mr. Tell.

"That sir," Buckram raised his glass, "would be my greatest pleasure." He let the orange brandy wet his upper lip, then set it down again.

Mrs. Tell was lecturing Lizzie and Mrs. Brookes on the writings of Samuel Johnson, Francis Barber's deceased benefactor.

"So it's all Dr. Johnson's money, then?" asked Mrs. Brookes, awestruck. "They've none of their own, Francis and Betsy?"

Mrs. Tell nodded and shook her head at the same time.

"Why, that's terrible," clucked Lizzie. "A man of his age, with children, too. *Quelle horreur!* What do you think, Buckram? Shouldn't a man, by honest toil alone, support his own family?"

"That's as it should be," said Buckram, barely registering her comments. He was busy scanning the gardens, ticking off points of potential conflict—the plain-clothed, freelance pressmen slowly counting through the gagglers under the hot-air balloon; the ecstatic, primal gasps from the nearby labyrinth of arbored walks; the long line of tense men standing silent by the Hairy Woman's tent, and the same at the White Negress's. Gravel paths were everywhere; a noiseless flight would be impossible. A pair of sword jugglers, a fire-eater, the bear-pit…"That's the way it is," he replied to whatever Lizzie had been preaching.

The women fell silent as the subject of their gossip appeared in the pavilion.

"Look what I've found!" Francis came strutting up from his shoeshine. His right hand pulled a toddler of mixed race. She had short, clumpy hair, torn up in places by someone's combing. Her face was a nest of worm eggs.

Huge, open sores wept down her neck and chest. A soft, happy spark twinkled from deep-sunken eyes.

"Found her kneeling by the river bank, lapping Thames water like a foal," Francis explained. "Seems to have taken a shine to me, the little urchin." He chucked her under the chin. "Truly it's as the poet said, 'From the strangest admixtures the greatest beauties grow.'" He glanced at his wife who was pursing her lips.

"Whaddye' say we take her for a swing ride and a feed of pease pottage?" he proposed.

Mrs. Brookes sniffed. "I was rather hoping to hear the operetta over a dish of oysters and cold collations."

The girl staggered up to Charlotte. "Mama," she cried, "Mama!"

Betsy sighed with ill-concealed relief.

"Awhhh, she thinks I'm her mother, poor thing." Charlotte smoothed her skirts down between her knees and let the thumb-sucking youngster burrow. "Poor thing," she murmured, dusting bugs from the child's head. "Poor thing, poor little thing."

A shower of rude laughter was moving through the Pleasure Gardens. It trickled across the Italianate rotundas, swept through the grottoes and beer lodges, gathered over the dicers and the sharps in the pagoda, and coursed down to the riverside pavilion.

A massive woman was striding through the crowd as if it were invisible. She reeked of soused herring and wore a patched cap, a patched dress, and a patch over one eye. She was barefoot, breathless, and quite white beneath her dirt-caked face. Rotting lungs rattled against her ribs every time she inhaled. She stamped across to the pavilion, looked left, then right.

"How now, my sweet?" She addressed the infant at Charlotte's waist. "Found favor in a new family, have yer!"

Her voice almost jolted Buckram from his seat. She bulked straight toward Charlotte and scooped up the child between her fleshy arms. She snarled chuckles at the horrified black women and shook the toddler at them.

"Mine!" she yelled in a broad Northern accent. "Not yours, she's mine. She is mine!"

Buckram felt his gonads shriveling far too rapidly. She turned to the massing sightseers who had followed her through the park. "Mine, mine, yes, mine!" she declared defiantly.

She turned to Francis and to Betsy. "This girl is mine. This is my daughter. Right?"

She turned to Buckram.

He wet himself.

Strangely enough, she was much bigger than before. Those shoulders, once full and straight, bowed and sloped under the weight of her enormous, dangling breasts. Nipples stood out against the fabric on either side of her navel. Now face to face, he noticed her split nose and her many missing teeth. Her single eye was compacted and bloodshot. It dilated, as did her nostrils, and was welling in recognition of the man before her, who echoed her petrification.

Her voice was unaltered and the lips hadn't changed. That was the very mouth that had once worked for him. It was fighting to find words.

"You...you...you...bastard!" shrieked Harriet. She shook her daughter at him. "You evil, black bastard!" The suffocating child warbled a wail.

Hullside Harriet pushed the wretched, sniveling infant in Buckram's face. "For all that we have and for all that's to come." She blew a sneer through clenched teeth, bathing Buckram's head in gin fumes. "That's what you said. You lyin' black arsehole. You're all the same, you dark men. Fook 'em 'n' forget 'em. Look at her! You don't you even know your own fookin' kid!"

The little girl struggled to escape her mother's mighty forearms, flailing her arms as if to swim to another's embrace.

"Mine?" Buckram choked.

"Look at you, a-quaffing in your fancy threads with your gang o' Sanchos, and your own blood penniless and two years starvin'." The strumpet bared her gums and tossed the bawling child into his lap.

The little girl pinched him. He wasn't dreaming.

"Your dadda," seethed Harriet. She nodded, savoring ancient hatred. "This is yer fookin' black sire, Cary-lass. Give 'im a good bite 'fore yer ol' ma gets one."

Harriet lunged, all teeth and nails, at her old lover's freshly soiled breeches.

Horrified, Buckram said, "Urrrrgh!" and toppled backward off his stool. He said it again as the girl fell from his arms and bounced one and a half times, knocking her head and hands against the pavilion's hard granite floor.

Harriet moved with unearthly speed, snatching wildly at Buckram's flailing ankles. He twitched frantically on the ground, between the bawling babe on one side and Harriet looming on the other.

The crowd in the pavilion was now afoot and staring at them. Charlotte, her mother and father and friends, were shocked speechless.

Harriet was standing over him, trying to kick his face.

"Buckram?" Charlotte, with a parent clutching each arm, was straining toward Harriet. "Buckram?" Her voice was high and trembling. "Do you know this dishclout?" she cried. "What is she saying? Who is she? Who is she?"

Onlookers cheered as Harriet's huge, hardened heel connected with Buckram's jaw.

Buckram pulled himself onto his knees and elbows. He closed his eyes, covered his head, and let himself be kicked.

There was nothing he could say or do. The child was theirs, his and Harriet's, he knew it in his blood. He was the father of Carol (feeling the name stick in his mind, he knew it would forever stick in his throat), an English girl, a white woman's child, and Charlotte, through her tears, could see his promises and his past, now torn and corrupted, for the living lies they were.

Beadles were approaching, press-gangs converged, Mrs. Tell had fainted. Buckram had no purpose here. He was a victim, a target, object of the world's derision and subject to his own, errant will.

He fled through the pleasure garden, punching a path through officials and bystanders, gaining comfort from his desperation now that the world had redrawn his goal. He was running to freedom. Running away, running to freedom. Running alone. Back to the wished-for brotherhood of men; the innocent, undemanding planet of play where, unjudged, he could wallow in his unrealized destinies and, unwanted, he could flounder and nurse his wounded pride.

Four trained hares, with drumsticks strapped to their paws, sounded his newest retreat from reality with their rhythmless beat on an old kettledrum.

His last memory: Harriet lumbering up behind him with a tulip-chewing girl-child under one arm, and, from somewhere behind them, the unmistakable racket of a Punch and Judy show.

London, 2 August 1786

The body of Mr. Neville Franklin, late of the Parish of St. Giles and also of Wilmington, Virginia, was discovered by the watch in Clare Court at three o'clock one Sunday morning.

His throat had been cut and his upper body badly bruised. He was buried in the cemetery at St. Giles's churchyard. Only friends of the church were present at the funeral. William and Buckram were far too busy to attend.

London, 17 August 1786

It was a warm, breezy day—a hanging holiday—so they had Oxford Street to themselves.

The ruts in the road were filled with sticks and straw, and when they rode over them, Buckram enjoyed reining the two bay mares and letting the big, gaudy stagecoach jounce across the ruts on its springy, new chassis.

William, leaning halfway out of the rattling carriage, shouted to him, "Slow down, Buckie, whoooa! Don't draw so much attention to us! Remember, we're supposed to be royalty!"

Both William Supple and Georgie George were dressed as African nobles in loose-flowing kente cloth of black, red, gold, and green. Buckram and the triplets wore similar loud livery tailored to European styles as befitting a driver and footmen. Every individual surface on the coach was painted either glossy green, glossy brown, or glossy sky blue.

Buckram sucked his teeth. Even in congested traffic such a carriage full of arguing black men would be the most conspicuous vehicle in the capital. He ignored his friend's words and cracked his whip, setting the horses off at almost a hand-gallop.

With some skill, he negotiated the turn into Duke Street, then reined the mares stiffly to a short, neat stop.

This was the approach to Grosvenor Square, their point of no return. Buckram sensed a cool, grim mood descend over him and his companions. They'd become soldiers again, moving through a plan and geared to their goal. All possible maneuvers had been discussed and confirmed. They were all on their own now, locked in their own separate roles, and there was nothing left to say. Not even "good luck." Time for action.

Hercules, Newton, and Charles jumped out to join Buckram at their places, fore and aft atop the coach, their faces settling into masks of unblinking sobriety.

Buckram waited, thoughtless in the silent street, seeing only how the shadows of its single tree—an ash—dappled softly across the smooth, handsome walls of some rich person's property.

Georgie George called out, "Forward!" and the coach set off toward Grosvenor Square.

Buckram willed the horses to an easy pace and relaxed, taking in the glorious architecture of this most modern place. He marveled at the flat but comely facades, the unity of design, the propriety of their disposition. There were no dunghills in the road, no boozed-up vagrants slouched against walls. An oval-shaped garden, sterile and undisturbed as a German park, sat in its center. Here there were pavements, fresh air, light, and space, and he felt exactly like what he was: an imposter, a black thief with evil intent.

He made two circuits of the square as agreed, checking for watchmen, bailiffs, soldiers—any armed white males. But today the greater part of London was on the other side of town, at Newgate, depending on a hanging for their pleasure.

The coach pulled up at No. 9 on the northeast corner where a thirteen-starred, thirteen-striped flag flicked lazily in the afternoon breeze. It was the American Embassy in London.

A pudgy footman fussed about in the street, waiting for the arrivals to disembark.

Buckram remembered Georgie's instructions, "Posture, posture! You're servant to a king. Eyes always forward, back straight, shoulders out. Never look back."

He felt Newton and Hercules dismount and open the carriage door. The coach rose and dipped twice as Georgie George and William Supple disembarked.

Buckram saw it in his mind's eye; the American footman—probably some no-hoper ex-pimp impressed from Trenton, New Jersey—ushering the house guests, with contemptuous ceremony, to the front door.

It all happened wordlessly. Buckram heard a door slam, he heard it being locked and bolted. He looked across at Hercules and met an equally raised pair of eyebrows.

There was one other person in the square, rounding the corner by the garden. An overexcited child, whipping his hoop back onto the yellowing grass.

Something was wrong, thought William. It was all wrong. He sensed this the moment the embassy's large, polished door clicked shut behind him.

There were too many people in the house. A handful of serving maids, Georgie had said. Nothing had prepared him for the commotion about them in the foyer. House servants—he counted at least seven—shuttled from room to room. An argument raged in the kitchen below stairs. Somewhere above, a girl was complaining loudly to her mother about her limited choice of clothes.

"Oh, mother, puh-lease, nobody wears a zone in London. Everyone's always laughing at us. Why do we have to be so *démodé?*"

"Nabby, you will wear exactly what Catherine has laid out for you. It's the latest fashion from Boston. The choice of all the quality young ladies."

"Mommmeee!"

Every few seconds a door on the right side of the foyer opened and a rude-featured man looked them up and down and scoffed openly. The man was plump, hot-checked, and blue-eyed; if Georgie hadn't given them a prior description of Minister Adams, William would have mistaken him for a typical "John Bull" Englishman.

William began to sweat under his heavy, voluminous clothes. He quelled his mounting discomfort with thoughts of the two letters he carried in his briefs. The first letter was a missive from Mary. It had been hand delivered two days earlier by a white clergyman recently arrived from the colonies. The good preacher—ordained in the Countess of Huntingdon's Connection (Mary's new church)—had spent a whole week tracking William down. His disapproval at finding him ensconced in the Charioteer was evident. William briefly recalled the shame he felt at inviting the man over the threshold and how his attempts at hospitality were gently refused. The preacher was keen to be on his way, and William had struggled to hide his relief at his swift departure.

The news was good, despite Mary's terse, remonstrative

style. She had moved back to New York with the children and was living near Wall Street where she was making a living as a seamstress. Their poverty was extreme, but, with God's help, they were able to make ends meet. Phillip and Nehemiah were receiving regular religious instruction, and they prayed for the day when they would be reunited with their father. She hoped that Buckram and Neville were in good health and prospering as much in their respective occupations as he was in his. (How was the London theater these days?) Gullah was dead—killed by a bout of the "king's evil." Almost everyone she knew in the free black community in New York was planning to emigrate to Nova Scotia. She requested money and asked how the weather was in London. She hoped he would inform them of his plans at the earliest opportunity. And she sent him all their love.

William had locked himself in his room, all the better to indulge himself in an hour of weeping, after which he composed his reply:

> *Dearest wife,*
> *Description would but beggar the joy felt on receipt of your good news. Good Mary, many were the nights I passed in deepest gloom, beset by thoughts of your travails, and my heart is well pleased to learn of your untiring efforts to maintain our little ones in the ways of rectitude. Acquainted as you are with the ways of our former masters, I trust you do bend their young minds ever toward the written word. It will stand them in good stead in that land where ignorance*

is the best and only security for obedience. Send both my love and fondest regards.

I am greatly dismayed to hear of the passing away of my old companion Gullah. I fear we will never again see his like, but I pray that his spirit is now at peace with the God of the Mother Country. It now falls upon me to relate an equal misfortune. Our good friend, Neville Franklin, has also found final rest. Alas, murder is suspected. Black life is almost as cheap in London as in the colonies, Mary. But we struggle on nonetheless. Friend Buckram is the same as always and asks after you constantly.

As for myself, I am greatly changed, and all for the better. Dear Mary, I fear I must confess a change of heart. You will forgive my inconstancy when I inform you of my good fortune. My appearances on the London stage continue apace and I have recently come to the end of another successful season on the boards of the Theatre Royal, Drury Lane. (Were it not for the constant and unfathomable popularity of the "Moor of Venice," I would surely starve!)

Now to the good news. A new production is afoot and I have been chosen to play the lead role. The title of the piece is "The Incomparable World." It is a radical new work, bound to revolutionize the stage. The author, a Mr. George George (rum name, eh?), is a renowned wit and man about town. This venture will, I believe, be the first to address the concerns of our benighted

people, both here and in the Americas. It is the-
ater of the highest order, and considerable sums
of money have been pledged toward its successful
execution. On completion of said play, it is my
firm intention to return to the American States
and be once more by your side.

My darling, I regret to say that this city has
changed, and I with it. Much ill feeling has grown
against the black folk who sojourn here and, as I
write, schemes are in motion to rid the Kingdom
of us via some great "African Resettlement." I
know not where this will lead but, suffice to say,
there can be no home for us here. Not for the first
time (or, dare I say, the last), I bow to your judg-
ment and have decided that we shall go to Nova
Scotia, there to seek our fortunes. Money shall be
no problem, believe me.

I bid you farewell now, beseeching you to
know that our separation and suffering is but
temporary and that all too soon, God willing, we
will be together as man and wife. Till then, with
all my love.

Your husband and faithful servant,
William Supple, Esq.

This letter, still unposted, lay nestled with Mary's correspondence, where it steadily absorbed the perspiration from
his thigh. He would now have to mail it from Plymouth, if
all turned to the good in the next twenty-four hours. That
would also be the best time to inform Georgie of his change

of plan. His ticket, however, was already booked for Recife, and the thought of making his way alone from Brazil to New York induced a fear almost as great as that of failing in this exploit only to dangle at the end of a hangman's noose.

He took small comfort from the two loaded pistols bandaged to his chest and the poignard strapped to his calf. Georgie, Newton, and Charles were similarly equipped. They were outnumbered, but at least they weren't out-gunned. That didn't help, though; the truth was he was scared for his life as never before.

It was the voices, he realized, American voices—that stream of mellifluous, bossy yelps calling from floor to floor and seeming to increase in volume as the space between the speakers diminished. Voices from a land without frontiers. His master's voice.

He felt four years old again, back on the auction block in Charleston, being examined by businesslike eyes and callous hands.

He looked at Georgie George. The man was ashen-faced and expressionless. Impossible to read his mind.

News of their arrival had filtered through the building and, one by one, members of the household, each on phony errands, trooped past to gape.

Presently, a black man came on the scene. He was a fat, bald butler. He directed them, without any acknowledgment whatsoever, through a pair of double doors to a large, high-ceilinged room that William knew to be the dining room of state.

"Wait here," he said. He closed the doors, leaving them alone again.

A massive mahogany table, capable of seating fifteen people, occupied most of the room. Above it hung a huge chandelier. The walls were decorated with framed paintings of pastoral licentiousness. A rear window gave onto a small, unkempt garden.

William made to speak but Georgie silenced him with a gesture. The Beggar King went to the front window to survey the square and to check on Buckram and Hercules.

"Time," he commanded.

Charles whipped out a fob watch. "Twelve fourteen," he said.

Georgie cursed sharply. They were ten minutes behind schedule. William felt himself beginning to panic. Buckram was under orders to intervene physically if they didn't reappear after twenty minutes. It would be just like him to do something rash at this stage.

Three pairs of footsteps sounded in the foyer, walking toward the dining room.

"Let's get this over quickly," whispered Georgie. His voice quavered. "No dramatics. Everyone to their posts."

No dramatics, thought William. My God, the man's a fool.

They faced the door in two ranks of two, Georgie beside William, behind them Charles and Newton with the small campaign chest.

The black butler opened the doors for two obviously rich but roughly dressed and unwigged white men.

"Mr. Hayden Irving," he announced. "And Mr. Tom Palmer."

As the doors were closing again, William noticed the footman and another fellow sidling up to stand guard, one on either side, in the foyer. He stiffened himself, trying to look more regal than petrified.

"Chief Kwaku," said Irving, "an honor to make your acquaintance." The slaver inclined his head gracefully but did not move to take William's hand. He was a burly man who looked as if he'd just stepped from behind a plough. He had extraordinarily large teeth over which his lips had difficulty closing; it was hard to tell if he was wincing with pain or beaming for joy. William let his eyes fall on the mouth again. The teeth were strong, white, and shiny. They were simply too large for his gums, and it dawned on William that they were not his own—they'd once belonged to a black man.

"I see you are admiring the Minister's chandelier," said Irving.

William was trying not to stare at the teeth.

"A fine example of French crystal, is it not? A souvenir from Mr. Adams's sojourn in Paris."

William grunted in what he hoped was a convincingly royal African manner.

"If you will permit," interjected Georgie, "Chief Kwaku is not conversant with the English tongue. I will officiate as his interpreter."

"No need, my friend, no need," gushed Irving. "In expectation of such a circumstance I have invited my associate, Mr. Tom Palmer here, to act in such a capacity. He is a long-time resident of the Gold Coast and fluent in all the major languages and dialects of that area. Mr. Palmer?"

The second American was a sallow-faced individual dressed in an old-fashioned, pleated coat with deep cuffs.

The tune "Yankee Doodle" came to William's mind. Mr. Palmer cleared his throat and licked his lips.

"*Kwaku Iha, orongona ikeni boyo-se. Numuni awa-se ngbonye!*"

William froze. Beside him, Georgie laughed gently.

"It is our custom, Mr. Palmer, that none but the appointed officials, in this case, my good self, may address his Highness directly. We are guests in this country and therefore wish to conduct our affairs in the corresponding tongue, if you please."

"As you wish," squeaked the linguist. He smiled weakly and furrowed his brows. He looked beaten and forlorn; if William had a bag of sweets he would have offered it to him.

Hayden Irving harrumphed and interjected, "Perhaps you gentlemen would like to get straight to business. Please be seated."

William and Georgie pulled out chairs at the corner of the table. Charles and Newton remained standing, their eyes firmly on the campaign chest.

Irving went to the door and rapped on it thrice. The two footmen dragged in a large iron strongbox, placed it near the top of the room, and retreated to their places out in the foyer.

"This, I believe, will prove sufficient indication of our intent to conclude our discussions successfully." Irving worked a key in the lock while beckoning George and William to inspect the contents.

The lid creaked. Refracted, flickering light sparkled up from the box onto their hungry, hovering faces. They looked down with mounting disbelief at a little girl's treasure trove of baubles, colored glass, redundant muskets, mirrors, beads, and trinkets.

"Fucksters!" spat Georgie.

"I beg your pardon?" said Palmer.

"Fucksters," Georgie repeated in an entirely American voice devoid of any emotion. He was erect and facing the two white men with a pistol in his hand. William stifled a yell. Newton and Charles had also drawn firearms. With some difficulty, William extricated his own weapon from beneath his robes.

"You two," barked Georgie. "Step aside."

They complied.

Georgie stepped backward to the strongbox and ran his hands through the worthless trinkets. Shaking his head, he threw handful after handful to the floor. He cleared several layers of the rubbish away then looked into the box and grunted. He drew out a bar of solid gold.

"How much of this d'you have?" He directed the question to Irving.

The slave trader was immobile. His nostrils quivered and a vein pulsed blue and angry above his neckerchief.

"How much?"

Irving's mouth worked desperately trying to shape words but no sound followed. Georgie nodded briskly at William.

Without pausing to think, William flipped his pistol, caught it by the barrel, and bashed Irving's dentures.

The man crumpled to his knees holding his face with both hands, his sob rising to a low howl. Georgie kicked him in the head. "No noise, understand?" Using his whole body, Irving nodded.

Palmer was inching toward the door.

"*Msetwe,*" he muttered, cupping his hands.

"*Msetwe Iba, fa bono.*"

The two Africans tittered.

"You. I'll ask you the same question," said George. "What's the gold worth?"

"*Korombenne wa fushoa, Iba.*"

Georgie shook his head and said, "Boys, make him talk English."

Charles flicked open a razor.

"*Msekwe,*" squealed Palmer. He lunged for the door and fell against the handle as a bullet splashed some of his brain against the woodwork.

For a few seconds the shot was the only sound in the house, in the square, and, seemingly, in the streets of the city beyond.

The door, pulled ajar by Tom Palmer's collapse, creaked open. A startled footman stared through the widening gap at the smoking pistol in William's fist. He looked down and saw Palmer's hand, in its frilly cuff, twitching by the base of the door. And there was Mr. Irving cowering in the corner, fingering his broken, bloody mouth. The footmen both drew pistols and ran to the center of the foyer shouting out the alarm to the entire house.

"The door," Georgie said calmly. "Secure it. Use the table."

The Grenadier Guardsmen jumped into action, kicking chairs out of the way and walking the heavy table in short, awkward pivots to the door.

"William, go and help them. Hurry!"

William tried to loosen his grip on the pistol but his hand and forearm were seized with incredible cramps. Still holding the useless weapon, he helped haul the table to the door and jam it under the handles.

"Listen to me, you in there!" The voice from the foyer could only have come from a man who styled himself Minister Plenipotentiary.

"Listen to me, I demand the immediate release of the American citizens, Hayden Irving and Tom Palmer. You are in illegal occupancy of these premises. You will surrender yourself to my marines at the count of ten. One...two..."

As the count began, Georgie seemed to compose himself all the more. "Newton," he ordered, "ready your lucifers. Charles, get out a couple of the big bangers. William, come carry the strongbox with me. We're leaving by the window."

"What are you doing, mister?"

The boy with the hoop sat cross-legged by the embassy wall and watched Buckram and Hercules lug a fat little cannon, the size of a bull terrier, from the carriage onto the pavement at great speed. It had all started when something like a firework had gone off in the building. Secretly, he hoped that it was a gunshot he'd heard and that it was nasty, ugly Nabby Adams who'd been murdered.

"What are you doing?"

"We're playing a game," Buckram replied breathlessly.

He crouched down, almost to the ground, and took a sight along the length of the barrel. "Right a fraction."

Hercules tapped the cannon round to the correct position.

"Are you a chocolate-man?" the boy asked.

"Yes," said Buckram, angling the weapon with one hand while fishing for matches with the other.

"Perfect. Front door lined up."

Hercules tamped down the preloaded powder and dropped in a ball.

"Taper ready?" asked Hercules apprehensively.

"Ready!"

The dining room window was being raised. Buckram dropped the slow-burning taper and rolled across the pavement. He jumped in the carriage through its open doors and out the other side, grabbing one of the loaded pistols from the seat on his way.

He turned swiftly round the back of the coach to face the window, holding the pistol at arm's length in a firing stance. Georgie and William were hefting a bulky iron box onto the window sill. They called for help in frenzied whispers.

"Herkie!" yelled Buckram, moving back to the little cannon. "I'm going to the window. Cover me."

Hercules gave him the thumbs up from his position upon the top-box. His musket barrel swiveled from the door to the first-floor windows and back again.

"Can I play, mister? Please."

"Why yes, son," said Buckram, suddenly inspired.

"See this?" he picked up the smoldering, smoky taper. "Our white friends will be coming through that door any second now. As soon as you see it open just a little, incywincy, eeny-teeny bit you're going to put this hot part onto this bit and make everyone laugh. All right, lad?"

"Ah, wow!"

"And mind you stand well back now. She jumps, sometimes."

Buckram ran to the window. William and Georgie were

only just managing to balance the strongbox over the sill. He noticed that William was carrying a spent pistol in his hand. There was a thud and a short scrape of wood on wood from deep inside the room.

"Willie, hold your end down," said Buckram. "It's too heavy a load to come over my side at once like this. Drop your gun. You're covered."

"He can't drop the gun. He's in shock," said Georgie.

"Oh, Jesus Christ."

Buckram heard another thud, this time louder, and saw an enormous table jammed under the door handles bump a quarter inch into the room. Newton guarded the entrance with two pistols. Charles held a lighted taper in his teeth and juggled two grenades.

"Buckie, take the weight on your shoulders. I'm coming out to your side. Hurry!"

Buckram put his back to the wall and felt the massive container slide onto his neck. "Wait!" he hollered, straightening his shoulders and redistributing the burden.

Georgie skipped through the window and landed gracefully beside him. They pulled together.

"William, you can let go now. Here, let it fall. There's nothing to break. We can drag it from here."

They let it clunk to the ground.

Buckram looked back inside. An ax was being applied to the doors. Something shifted the light at the far side of the room. He looked again. Through the rear window, a shadow shimmered and vanished against the garden wall.

"Charlie! In the garden! They're in the garden! Grenade! Now!"

With the taper between his lips, Charles kissed the round, black, metal bomb. "Everybody down!"

He flung it with full force at the window. In the garden the black butler sprang up with a leveled musket. He was practically vaporized in the storm of shrapnel from the dull explosion.

"Who did he think he was," said Georgie, "Crispus Attucks?"

Dust clouds breezed in through the shattered window frame. The door resounded to renewed shoulder charges. Ax blows rained down on it in frantic succession. The table had shifted out three inches.

"Come, brethren, let us flee!"

Charles and Newton hopped through the front window and helped Buckram carry the gold to the coach. Once inside the vehicle they started shedding their African costumes and wriggled into everyday apparel.

"Willie-boy, move, we're going," called Georgie.

"One second," said William absently, "I nearly forgot something." He pulled his second pistol from his robes and shot Mr. Irving between the eyes.

"Better now?" asked George incredulously.

"Much."

"Good. Then we're away."

It was only as they boarded the coach that William noticed a child standing by the small cannon holding a lighted taper. Buckram was passing him two fresh twists and demonstrating how to light one with another. Buckram leapt up onto the driver's perch and cracked the whip.

"Thanks, sonny," he chirped. "It's a good game. Don't forget now, she jumps."

"And everyone will laugh, won't they?"

"Oooh yes! We all will. Lots. Later."

"Goodbye, Mr. Chocolate-man!"

He whipped the horses to a gallop down Upper Grosvenor Street. A whoop went up from inside the carriage. They swept diagonally across a trafficless Tyburn Lane and cut into Hyde Park.

"There's Henry with the fresh horses!" said Newton. The ex-Guardsman pointed up the dusty avenue toward a reservoir shrouded behind trees. Henry Prince was standing akimbo atop a smart but austere mailcoach. He looked unrelaxed yet very pleased to see them coming.

All seven men unloaded the "royal carriage." Their flashy clothes were bundled, weighted with cannon balls and dumped into the reservoir. The horses were slapped away to canter free into the marshes of Hyde Park, dragging their coach behind them.

As the strongbox was being lowered into the mailcoach's false compartment an unmistakable boom! carried over from the direction of Grosvenor Square.

"Now there's a useful young fellow," jested Georgie. They were laughing so much that no one noticed Buckram unsheathing his old sword-pistol.

"Well, brethren, let's quit this land," Georgie turned to be hailed by the company. His eyes flashed once, almost imperceptibly as they caught Buckram's stance. "To Plymouth," he continued, holding the door open for his cronies. "And Mr. Supple, give us a tune, a new song. A victory march!"

William worked up a jaunty air into which strands of

both "Yankee Doodle" and "London Bridge Is Falling Down" were woven.

"Hop aboard, Buckie," said Georgie. He was staring at the sword-pistol with untroubled eyes.

William's music stopped as the realization of what was happening took hold of the coach.

Buckram had the weapon aimed at Georgie's chest.

"Time's up, Georgie George," he said.

"I thought my time was just beginning. What's this now?"

"This is a loaded pistol. George, I should have done this a long time ago."

"Buckie," reasoned the Beggar King, "don't pull that trigger."

"Why not? What have I to lose?"

"Two thousand English pounds of solid gold. Don't you care about that?"

"You've no idea how much I don't care," growled Buckram. "It was you all along, wasn't it?"

"Now look," said Georgie. "The alarm has gone out and our lives are at stake should we tarry here. So, I beg you, please shoot or shut up."

"I'll shoot, I'll talk, and I'll take my time about it."

Georgie raised a hand to quiet the crew in the coach.

"It was you who had Neville murdered. We all know that," Buckram ranted.

"Wouldn't there be better times and places for this discussion?"

"No."

"Very well, very well. So I'm a murdering madman and I deserve to die. Shoot me." Georgie bared his breast.

Buckram squeezed the trigger. There was no explosion. A wisp of smoke snaked from the barrel of the firearm.

Georgie stroked his chin. "I didn't credit you with such strength of will. Well, now that's over, shall we depart?"

"No, no, no, it's impossible." Every muscle in Buckram's body seemed to tremble. He was squinting hard at Georgie and stepping backward, away from the mail-coach. "So, it's true—what Neville said. It's true, then. You are the de…"

"Will you shut up!" screamed Georgie. Quite leisurely he reached into the coach and withdrew an enormous double-barrelzed flintlock pistol. "Let me explain," he continued, cocking the hammer. "Knowing your weapon to be loaded, I greased the flint with goose fat. This gun is fully opera-tional, you will find. So I beseech you, a third time, get in or go your own way."

Buckram flung down his sword-pistol and threw up his arms.

"Your game again, Georgie. It's always your game."

He saluted William and the triplets, then turned his back on the coach and walked with slumped shoulders through the cover of trees into the marshland beyond.

"He doesn't know what he's doing," said William. "I'll go after him. We can't leave him here."

"Willie, save your strength. He's gone, can't you see?" He tapped the side of his head twice. "Let's get away while we still can. You've still a family to look out for, and don't for-get, you're a rich man now. Rich men don't die for nothing."

"No, wait, just one second."

William tossed a dozen or so of the smaller ingots into a canvas bag and ran to catch up with Buckram.

"If your heart's set on misery, it's better that it be monied."

Buckram accepted the bag and slung it over his shoulder.

"It's a very small world we live in, Buckram." William held out his hand. "Until we meet again."

"God be with you, William Supple. Give my regards to Mary and the lads. Until we meet again."

They shared a weak, confused handshake then Buckram stumbled off west to where the park grew wildest.

William watched from the coach as his friend tramped off toward the higher grass and rougher ground. He watched as Henry Prince cracked the whip and the heavy coach jerked them away.

Buckram became a speck on the horizon. He could have been anyone or nobody, heading through the strands of waving green and, maybe, turning round to give a final salute.

Brazil, Recife, October 1786

A cool, steady breeze carried a flight of macaws over the palm fronds along the beach. William Supple took another deep breath and let his body sink beneath the water for the fifth time. The sea here was neither green nor brown: it was clearest blue.

He opened his eyes and saw flotillas of multi-colored fish swarm about in rainbow abandon. He floated an inch or so below the ocean's surface, enjoying the salt water's soothing sting against his mosquito-ravaged skin.

His lungs were close to bursting, but he was being seduced by the ebb and flow of the greater currents into which he was being drawn. Then it came to him, almost as a sweet realization. I could die here. Not such a bad place to die. Suspended here off this perfect tropical coast. Just another naked brown corpse drifting away from this hot, humid, beerless country. He pictured his cadaver at the mercy of the tides, floating forever between the Old World and the New, never sinking, never rising, and never touching either shore.

It would be far better to die thus than to perish on Brazilian soil. Far better. In his short time in this place he had come to learn one thing: Brazil was the worst place on God's earth!

He had been a fool. Georgie George had led him to a hellhole beyond his wildest imaginings. Recife was a nightmare town; worse than London in midwinter, worse than Carolina come harvest time. Every shop assistant owned slaves, every woman, black and white, was for sale. Priests outnumbered paupers. The whole port basked in evil. The enormity of the horror had struck William from the moment the little packet brig docked by the quayside. From his first view of the city, reason had abandoned him entirely.

Georgie laid a hand on his shoulder and steered him toward the gangplank.

"Be unafraid, William," he said in the same tone he might have used to request salt at the dinner table. "This is but the start of our journey. It will soon be a memory. Be unafraid."

William made to reply, but was possessed by a fit of hiccups. He wondered how Georgie's dreams of proud, free black cities (*quilombos* he called them), married up to the violent reality into which they were descending.

He let Georgie take his hand and lead him, as a father would a child, down the gangplank and onto dry land.

Black men were everywhere, legions on them. Half-naked and in chains, they trotted through the streets in whip-driven columns. William saw them laboring like mules at all points in the port: waist-deep in the water; shoring up walls and sandbanks; hauling massive blocks of stone uphill toward some new bridge, town house, or cathedral; lading and unlading ships' cargoes of coffee, rum, cotton, sugar, and gold. The stuff of empires—slave produce.

The two travelers had the greatest difficulty trying to move anonymously through the city. As far as William could see there were no free blacks in Recife. He and Georgie, apparently, were the only black people wearing clothes. Their outlandish styles and Georgie's metropolitan swagger attracted much attention from the good freemen of the port. William soon realized that his wealth was of no value in a city where the most cordial address they'd received was, "Negro, we will have you join us!"

Three soldiers had been trailing them from the harbor, walking five steps behind them, hissing lazy Portuguese curses. William saw them loosen the clasps on their scabbards just moments after they'd left the harbor.

"I think we might just need a little help here," said Georgie as they crossed a canal bridge. The bridge led to an alleyway that gave onto a square packed with people.

"Any ideas, Georgie?" William croaked. These were the first words he had managed to utter since disembarking. "Any ideas? Anything? Do you know where we're going?"

"Trust me, William. This must be the place."

What place?

A morning market was in full flow in the big square (*Praça da Independência,* William read). Stall keepers, hawkers, and peddlers, almost all with a slave or two in tow, took up most of the space. An enormous church decorated with carvings occupied one side of the square.

"We're nearly there!" Georgie shouted, pointing at the church. "If I'm not mistaken, that's the *Igreja de Santo Antonio.*"

"The what?" William could almost feel the soldiers' breath on his neck. He heard them trailing their drawn blades against masonry and imagined the showers of sparks this excited.

"Follow me. Quickly. This way," said Georgie. His eyes

flicked across the crowd as if searching for a friend. "Come," he commanded. "It's time to run."

They tore off through the market, weaving through the stalled shoppers in a vain attempt to shake off the sword-wielding soldiers. William was tempted to drop his gold-heavy canvas bag on the cobbles to ease his flight, but he hadn't come through three years of trials simply to die penniless. If he was to be murdered, he resolved, it would be with his bag of loot clutched to his chest.

They were approaching a tavern a few doors down from the church; its name was posted in English above the door, The Eagle's Nest. William recognized several deckhands from the packet brig among the drinkers seated outside.

"Ahoy, me buckos!" yelled Georgie as he ran toward them.

"Ahoy!" came the massed, if hesitant, reply. The sailors, seeing the cause of their ex-passengers' distress, rose as one. Their hands flew to their weapons, and the soldiers stopped in their tracks. Georgie and William disappeared into their ranks and didn't stop running until they had reached the back room of the tavern.

"My God!" William fought to catch his breath. "Our lives have been saved by English sailors!"

"And don't you forget it," Georgie advised. "They won't. Like it or not, this is an English inn and we are English speakers. Until we blacks use our original African language, our lives are linked with these people and theirs with ours." He lectured on: "We are in Brazil. To these seafarers, it matters less that we are black men than that we have a common tongue. Whenever you find yourself outside the English-speaking world you will be reminded of this, William."

"D'you mean to say that the same thing would happen were these men Carolina rebels or slavers newly arrived from Africa?" William spat the words.

"Yes," Georgie replied, thoughtfully. "I believe it would. Indeed, some of these men are slavers, no doubt. Come. Let's meet them and study their ways."

William shook his head and shouldered his bag. Georgie was a deep one for sure. How he'd survived was a mystery. For the longest time he'd reasoned that Georgie George had succeeded in wooing luck from sheer, willful naïveté, or that his confidence (as awesome as it was congenial) was woven from multilayered, ever changing strategies. What was becoming clearer under the brighter light and sharper shadows of this country, was that Georgie had gone mad a long time ago, maybe in London, or maybe in the colonies where he'd been driven (so it was said) to murder another black man for the sake of adopting his crazy double Christian name. But Georgie was no sadblack. His insanity seemed anchored and without anguish; it flourished and gave seed to all with whom it came into contact. William envied him.

There were a good twenty or so men drinking in The Eagle's Nest. Most of them were now filing into the back room to welcome Georgie and William. They were a swarthy, rough-hewn crew, Englishmen too long abroad, drowning their sorrows while waiting for another ship to take them from this friendless city.

"You're all right now, lads. The Porto boys have gone. Took one look at us, then..." The tiny, bearded tar blew air through his teeth and flicked a wrist. "You're among friends here."

"We owe you our lives," Georgie intoned.

"Oh, I don't know about that. You owe us nothing more than a good drink, I'd say."

"Well," William said. "Drinks for all, then. To your good health!"

Although he addressed the company, his entire attention was trained on a single individual—a large, jolly-looking black man who returned his stare with an inquiring smile. The face was familiar, but William couldn't place it. He noticed Georgie's silence and unusually tense manner.

"I know you, don't I?" ventured the black seaman. "You're from London, aren't you?" His gaze jumped between their faces, and William took his cue from Georgie and said nothing. He was sure he'd crossed paths with this stranger before, but where? when?

The sailor stepped up to Georgie and stared directly into his face.

"Yes," he stated. "I do know you." His voice dropped several registers. "London, St. Giles. Drury-side. That black man's ken in Brydges Street, the Charioteer. That's where I know you from."

"Maybe," said Georgie flatly.

"The name is Julius, friends. Julius Bambara."

"Well, brother Julius," said William. "What say we retire to the bar? What's your pleasure?"

"They've only spirits in this part of the world. Some wines, but mostly rum."

"No ale?" piped William.

"None," Julius replied.

"Well, rum for all, then."

Georgie held William's sleeve and pulled him backward while Julius left the room.

"That man is dangerous. I know him of old. He's a blab-bermouth."

"I have also seen him before, I think," William added. "Can't say where from, but I do know him."

"Beware, William. Watch your words."

The Eagle's Nest also served as a lodging house. Rows of triple-tiered bedding filled the four upstairs rooms. Some of the bunks held snoozing occupants. Georgie and William reserved bedspaces for themselves on the second floor and stowed their luggage as unobtrusively as possible before returning downstairs to join the party drinking their health.

William ordered a dinner. He kept one eye on the vast quantities of rum being consumed while the other was trained on Julius circling the room on a none too subtle course toward him. Georgie appeared to be enjoying himself with a band of privateers. William overheard him regaling them with unlikely stories of tobacco smugglers and customs men he had known back in New York.

At the mention of the colonies, William was suddenly assailed by a wave of anxiety and guilt. He took a long gulp from his bottle to stanch the painful sensations flooding his body. Images of his wife and children swam round his vision. This was no place for a husband and a father. What was he doing here? He needed more strong drink or perhaps a woman's company, maybe a visit to the church on the square. He needed sanctuary. His mind fluttered feebly along avenues of possible pleasures, but he had lost his appetite for excitement. His powers of self-delusion were spent.

"So, what ails you, brother?" Julius's face bobbed before William's. He was holding a bottle similar to his own.

"Just thoughts, friend. Errant thoughts."

Julius drew up a stool and perched beside him. "First time in Brazil?"

William nodded.

"Fine country, wouldn't you say?"

William was lost for words. The African seaman twitched frantically, jumping up from his seat and looking left and right out of the window. "I know just what you need. I was like that myself, first trip out here. Thinking much the same as you. Asking, 'What do the blacks here do for fun?' That's it, no?"

"Something like that," William conceded.

"Well, let me tell you, you'll have the time of your life out here. Stick with me. I'll show you some assemblies you'll not believe. Ever heard of Xango?"

"No," William lied. Thanks to Gullah's instruction, he was well acquainted with the Yoruba pantheon, but it wasn't a subject on which he felt this man could enlighten him.

"That's a rout and a half for you. I'm off there myself this evening. Just by the old market. Come with me, if you like."

William didn't answer.

"I recognize that look in your eye," said Julius. "It's homesickness. The old London longing. You must have been there some time."

"A few years."

"Great town, London. Best place in the world. D'you ever buck up with Frank Barber?"

"No. Never."

Julius's mouth dropped open in amazement. "How come?" he asked. "Everybody knows old Francis! He was a good bud of mine, y'know. Gave me a saying I'll never forget." Julius waited for William's prompt. It wasn't forthcoming, but he continued nonetheless. "When a man's tired of London, he's tired of life. For London hath in it all that the...the...oh, something or other. I forget. But it's true, tho', isn't it? Tired of London...tired of life. Me, I'm getting back out there first chance I get."

William was startled at the man's words. "You're going back?"

"That's what I said. Soon as I cadge a berth on an outbound vessel. That's where I'll be. Thameside. Back home."

Back home. Hot chestnuts and mulled wine—that's what they'd be selling in the Piazza right now. Logfires blazing a warm welcome from the windows of packed kens at every slushy corner of the Court End. Books, gambling parlors, high conversation, Stepney ale. William swallowed and looked at the platter of salt cod and potatoes being carried to his table by an old sea dog.

"I want you to do me a favor," he blurted. "When you get back to London, that is."

"I'll do what I can. Anything for a brother."

"There's a friend I'd like you to contact. I believe he resides there still. I want you to deliver a note, if you'll be so kind."

"I see no problem there. Who is this fellow? Where can I find him?"

"His name is Buckram."

Julius froze.

"Yes, just Buckram," William continued. "Nothing more. He can be found at the sign of the Charioteer, Brydges Street, Drury-side. You are familiar with it, I understand?"

"Familiar with both the place and the man."

"You know him?"

"Know him? Me and Buckie go back a long, long way. He's another old bud of mine. There's only one Buckram in this world. Tall fellow, prankster, wild card, good bud."

"That's Buckie, all right." William felt himself sigh with relief. "So you'll do me this service, then and carry a note for him. I'll pass it to you later this evening?"

"Why gladly. But a note?" Julius cackled. "Don't you know Buckram can't even read a sundial at the North Pole?"

"You may find he's changed," William snapped.

"Well, like I said, anything for a brother. It'll be my pleasure." Julius drained his bottle and banged it on the table.

"Another, friend?" William offered.

"And another and another." Julius smacked his lips. "Welcome to Brazil."

William prodded the leathery slab of fish and the water-logged potatoes. Outside the window, the sun was rising high above the bustling square. Some sort of fruit and vegetable market was in progress. Were it not for the cloudless sky and the squads of slaves fetching and carrying for every stall holder it would almost have resembled the Piazza at Covent Garden with the church to one side.

"What were you two gabbling about?" Georgie had appeared suddenly in Julius' seat.

"Nothing. Just the 'black life,' y'know."

"We have to leave this place. They'll be asking questions about us when they sober up in a day or so. Have you told that wretch anything about us?"

"Not a word."

"Good."

William placed a spoonful of potato in his mouth. It immediately dissolved to the consistency of semolina. Georgie started slapping out a jaunty beat—half military, half African—on his side of the table. Although it was a merry rhythm, William was aware of its growing pace and intensity. He sensed Georgie's stare settle upon him. It was a feeling akin to being drawn through a press.

"William."

William swallowed his bolus of potato and felt it slide down to his belly where it fizzed in a pool of rum. For the second time in his life, he looked directly into his friend's eyes. They were jet-black and seemingly without pupils. Or maybe nothing but pupils. He had never noticed this before. These are not the eyes of a mammal, he noted deliriously. An immense intelligence shimmered in those depths.

"William, I have known for some time now, since Plymouth in fact, that this is where we must part."

"Plymouth? What do you mean?"

"My friend, I saw you down at the docks there. You had a gift, you said, for Newton. A flask of gin, I believe. I followed you through the streets and your destination was the Exchange rather than any Halifax-bound boat. And there, if I am not mistaken, you passed a letter across the counter for postage overseas. I can only assume the letter was for your wife's attention. From your silence during the voyage and your behavior since landing I must take it that you will be heading for Nova Scotia some time soon. Leaving me to perish alone in some Amazon backwater, eh?" There was no anger in Georgie's voice. In fact, his face had its habitual smirk. "For an actor, you are cursed with a weak spirit, William Supple. Surely, you must have known I'd bear no ill will to your desire to be with your loved ones in a safe place. After all our times together I never suspected that you were actually afraid of me. You are tho', aren't you?"

William inclined his head slowly and sliced another potato with his spoon. "Afraid of you, Georgie?" he said. "Maybe. Yes, sometimes I think I am."

"Well, that makes two of us, then," said Georgie. He recommenced his table-top drumming, this time more softly.

"What are you going to do, Georgie? What about the *quilombo*? The black free state?"

"That is my dream, not yours, remember? It was never your intention to accompany me there. That you have voyaged thus far with me is a consequence of your own vacillation, but I thank you, nonetheless, for your companionship. You made a rough voyage all the smoother."

William made to protest, but Georgie silenced him, as only he could, with an upraised palm.

"I haven't been idle during our brief time on this shore. I am making travel arrangements for us both."

"Us!" William screeched.

"Yes," Georgie continued calmly. "There is a Dutch merchant ship bound for New York in two days' time. They have berths for a few passengers more. I think you should be one of them."

"But you? What'll you do, Georgie?"

"My journey will take me inland as planned. Tomorrow I'm to meet with an Indian guide. A good man, they say. He'll take me where I need to go."

For a short part of eternity neither man spoke.

"This is to be our last night together," Georgie announced. "Let's celebrate."

"Here? How?"

"In the old style. A night on the town."

"Julius mentioned some black hop down by the old market somewhere. What say we...?"

"No!" barked Georgie. "I have already accepted an invitation from our friend over there." He glanced toward the bar where a white sailor raised a drink in salute. "We'll be routing with them. It'll be safer. Should trouble arise, they can always claim we are their slaves, purchased in Barbados, eh?"

William tried to laugh, but tears welled in his eyes.

"Y'know, I'll miss you, Georgie George."

"Yes." Georgie blew a single, high clear note from the neck of his bottle. "I'll miss me, too." He shrugged himself out of his frock coat and let it fall to the floor. "Especially that old thing."

They drank.

Early the next day, before the town was awake, George shook William from his bunk and ordered him to collect his things. Still groggy from the night before, William took the letter to Buckram from his pocket and tiptoed over to Julius's bed. He placed it in the sleeping African's kit bag, then slipped out of The Eagle's Nest and into the mist-shrouded morning.

He followed Georgie across an empty *Praça da Independência*. A stout, copper-colored man was waiting for them on the steps of the church.

"William," said Georgie. "This is Hector. Hector, William."

The Indian grunted a greeting.

"He knows a place out by Olinda where you can stay till tomorrow. A fishing village some miles down the coast. It's safe. You'll be out of harm's way there."

They arrived at the little Indian settlement shortly before noon. It was just as Georgie had described it. Tranquil: no white faces. Georgie's last words to him as he saddled up a pair of mules for his journey were, "Whatever you do, William Supple, make sure you get on that boat for New York. This is no place for a man such as yourself. You are going to be very rich and very happy in cold, old Canada. Should you meet Charles and his brothers up there, be sure to give them my regards. Godspeed, William Supple. Godspeed."

Then he was gone. And William, alone and hung over, walked to the sea, shedding his clothes as he went.

William raised his head from the ocean and inhaled deeply. He shook himself from his morbid reveries. Two more voyages, he thought. That's all. Two more, then I'm home and free. He turned his back on the swelling currents gathering beneath him and started to swim back toward the shoreline. With each stroke he felt his strength returning, and, warming to the sensation, he swam all the harder. He knew now that he would survive, even as a farmer eking a living from the harsh Nova Scotian soil. No more acting for William Supple. No more noble, savage deaths on the white man's stage. Time to play himself, unscripted. He would triumph anew in his role as the good father and the good husband in a new world. And London Bridge could fall down without him.

London, 24 December 1787

Buckram stood by a snowman outside the door of the Charioteer and listened to the shouts and laughter of several people in the bright, drafty room. The alehouse was full this afternoon, and, through the frost-coated window, he watched Old Morris being chased round the tavern by a villainous-looking white man with a hot poker. Ten or so men, all white and wearing the all-in-green uniforms of the Queen's Rangers Hussars, caroused and cheered on the deadly game. Offaly Michael was still there. He sat glumly on a stool behind the bar, his arm in a sling.

It had been over a year since Buckram had taken a drink in a Drury-side alehouse. His breath steamed up the windowpane. A very drunk young soldier stared out at him, trying to ascertain if the well-built black man with a satchel was really wearing a fantail hat, a pigtail wig, and a triple-collared redingote greatcoat. Tacked to the wall above the soldier was Henry Prince's brown paper sketch of Georgie George. The Beggar King, with folded arms and head thrown slightly back, sneered imperiously down at the company. The sketch was plastered with the kisses and signatures of his forlorn female admirers. Buckram grinned.

Georgie, wherever he was now, wouldn't be seen dead in such a place, he was sure of it.

He stamped snow from his high-low boots and glanced at his gold fob watch. A quarter past four. He was late for work. Strangely enough, making a living and life in general had become easier since Georgie's and William's departure. Buckram's old bilker contacts had come in useful and had helped him, at some cost, to convert his small stash of gold ingots into common coin. With the proceeds and with Pete Fortune as his proxy, he had secured the lease on a poky, two-horse stable in Langley Street next to the smithy's. He even had enough money to employ Cato, the lipless young beggar, as a stablehand and dogsbody. Buckram kept a room in Wapping High Street, far from the temptations of the Court End. He ate regular meals and traveled by hackney cab. He dressed warmly and well. By his own efforts he had learned to read, write, and keep accounts. Where once he'd haunted taverns, he haunted booksellers. He read Sterne and Smollett. To his great surprise he'd come across a recently published pamphlet by Ottobah Cugoano entitled *Thoughts and sentiments on the evil and wicked traffic of the slavery and commerce of the human species.* He read the work in a single sitting, marveling at the sensation of holding in his hands the condensed thoughts of someone he had met face to face. He had never known such an eloquent, concise condemnation of the slave trade, and, reflecting on its words (as he did almost daily), he often felt compelled to join one of the radical groups or antislavery associations now springing up all over the city. But Buckram never made it to a political meeting. Business always beckoned him and business was good. But he was lonely. Never more so than now: the festive season. Family time. He walked away from the Charioteer and headed back to Langley Street. The roads were clogged with beggars and cripples of every description. On Russell Street he found himself waist deep in a sea of street urchins who reeked of gin. He batted them aside and stalked off toward the Piazza, trying to suppress the now familiar panic. It was the children's eyes, he realized; they had bored into him and tapped a stream of memory he'd long forced beneath his everyday horizon. All they demanded was a penny or two for their Christmas family meal. But he found himself unable to give. The sensation that seized him flushed out instantly to his limbs, carrying with it the threat of near paralysis. He forced himself to march across the Piazza through the graying snow and came to the corner of James Street where he halted, shivering anew in the grip of his unaddressed problem. There was a hole in his life— a Charlotte-sized hole—that the presence of children always brought to the fore.

Charlotte had given birth to a son and, for over a year, she had been living with her parents in Staffordshire; that much he had gleaned from his constant interrogation of Lizzie (the poorest keeper of secrets). From her he had obtained their address, and, since March of this year, he had posted a fortnightly stream of letters to Lichfield in which he implored his beloved to accept him back into her life or at least acknowledge his correspondence. It had been in vain. Finally, during the first week in August, he received a reply. The response was not from Charlotte. It was from her father. Buckram remembered how feverishly he'd broken the seal on that letter, and the strange mixture of joy and disappointment he'd experienced on reading its contents. It was a brief note in an artless hand written in turquoise ink and littered with random capitals. The family was faring well it said. The boy was in good health. And would Buckram be so kind as to visit Lichfield on the last Monday of the month to see his first-born?

Buckram's elation was unbounded and he spent the month preparing for his trip. On the day of his departure he set off on his black mare laden with gifts and hopes of redemption in the bosom of his family. It was not to be.

It was Mr. Tell alone who met him at the gates to the Stanford estate. From their first greeting it became evident that Mr. Tell—a man he dearly wished to call "father"— was to be the only adult family member he would meet that day. Mondays, he explained, found Mrs. Tell at the market and Charlotte at the village school in Burntwood some miles away. He had planned this as a meeting of males. There was no invitation to stay the night, and Buckram knew he would return to London alone and half-fulfilled.

It was a bonny child that Buckram held in his arms.

"His name is Hosea," Mr. Tell informed him. Buckram guessed this was a name chosen by Charlotte's mother. The happy brown child beamed up at his father. Buckram wallowed in the love pouring from the pair of great swallow eyes and heard his son gurgle k-k-k.

"My daughter is a very proud and unforgiving soul," said Mr. Tell. "She and her mother speak of naught else but you and that with shame and sorrow. Know that you may never be forgiven for your misdeeds. But there is always hope, Buckram. It will take time. Much time."

Buckram had time.

When the clock struck three Mr. Tell simply said, "Go, go now." Buckram left a sum of money and went on his way.

He mounted his mare and galloped off, but not to London. He reached Burntwood just before four o'clock. The schoolyard was empty, and Charlotte was nowhere to be seen. He waited for almost three hours, till darkness fell. She never appeared. They had missed each other by minutes, he realized.

But he had time.

On returning to London he flung himself into the world of commerce with renewed vigor. Business was brisk and there was money to be made. Here was a world large enough to absorb any man's energies. There were debtors to chase (thirteen) and creditors to avoid (two). He needed to find a hay merchant reliable enough to supply him through the cold spell. He had to learn how to unfreeze tallow (all horses stabled with him were guaranteed an "African Luster"). There were problems with Cato (was he inviting friends over to sleep on the premises?). But all his frantic bargainings and efforts to displace stress were to no avail. Charlotte and Hosea remained foremost in his mind.

Buckram braced himself against a cold wind sweeping down Long Acre and tramped on to his workplace. He hated Christmas—a solstice festival initiated by pagans, adopted by Christians, now waylaid by merchants. It was a week for solid burghers and their kin to congratulate themselves on their own survival in this coldest of months in this coldest of lands. It was Christmas Eve and the streets of London were empty except for solitary shoppers and hordes of the homeless. Vagabonds had wedged themselves into almost every doorway of Long Acre.

In an alley on the St. Giles side of the road, a band of destitute black men had made a shelter for themselves out of old timber and packing cases. They stood over a small, smoky fire and sang sea shanties as they passed round a jar of All Nations. One of their number held out a pewter cup to passers-by at the mouth of the alley. It was just as William Supple had said, Buckram reflected: there would always be black people starving about the streets of London. Every now and then there would be a public outcry, and demands for their expulsion would be followed by yet another cruel, half-baked scheme to drive them from the land. For two hundred years this had been their condition here. Would another two centuries bring any change?

As Buckram felt his pockets for spare coins he saw the beggar with the pewter cup crossing the road to address him. The man shivered constantly, even though he wore four layers of heavy clothes. His bushy hair and full beard were twisted into rough, ugly plaits. Instinctively, Buckram tilted his head to avert his gaze. He abhorred making eye contact with black tramps. More eyes, more pain, more memories.

"Beg a penny, brother. Beg a penny. Just one penny, sir." The stench from the beggar was that of old sweat and urine. Buckram held his breath as he extended his fistful of money.

"God bless you, brother. Thank you, thank..." The mendicant dipped his head into Buckram's line of vision, and Buckram felt every hair on his body stand on end. The face, now inches from his own, began to smile. And as it smiled, its features assumed a familiar configuration beneath all the crusty skin and hair.

"Buckram!" Julius Bambara beamed uncontrollably. "I knew I'd find you. They said you were still here. I've been searching for you since...since..." A tearful, terrified look flashed across his face. He grabbed Buckram's lapels. "I'm in trouble, Buckie-boy. Real trouble this time. You've got to help me. I haven't eaten for days. I'm near the end this time, I swear. Look, I've got something here." Julius began a frantic, fumbled search through his many pockets. "I've got something, something for you. No, wait!"

Buckram shrieked and shoved the crazy seaman aside. The last thing on earth he needed was another Christmas with Julius Bambara. He was too old for this kind of acquaintance. It would destroy him—the ever present promise of impermanence, the infinite fascination of self-hatred, the studied cultivation of vulgarity and suspicion. He had been there before, hostage to the world's weakness and his own. His soul craved rest and reconciliation, and there was only one place that could be found. He clutched his satchel to his side and marched stiffly down the street.

Julius was in no condition for a chase, hunger and influenza had sapped his strength. He hobbled after Buckram as best he could, but his well-dressed friend had vanished among the stables and workshops of Langley Street. He was nowhere to be found, and no footsteps were traceable in a street full of straw and horse manure.

He smoothed the creases out of William Supple's envelope and tore the letter in half, then into quarters, eighths and sixteenths. "To the devil with you!" he growled. He flung the shreds to the icy wind and watched them flutter and fall to the filthy ground.

Cato was playing cribbage and enjoying a Christmas cheroot with the blacksmith's apprentice when Buckram came bursting through the door.

"I thought I told you. No smoking!" Buckram whipped the cigar from the stablelad's mouth with his left hand while his right swept up at an ear-clipping angle. Cato ducked deftly under the blow. The smith's apprentice, seeing the expression on Buckram's face, stubbed out his cheroot on his leather apron and slunk back to his workplace.

"And get that thing out of here!" Buckram kicked the cribbage box, sending the tiny pins flying into a loosened bale of hay. "This isn't a gaming house! Any callers?"

Cato shook his head.

"No work to do, boy?"

Cato hunched his shoulders and looked across the quiet stable. The only occupant was Juno, Buckram's horse. Accounts aside, there'd be no more business today.

"Make yourself busy, lad. Polish up my best tack and saddle the mare."

The stableboy nodded briskly and set to work with beeswax and ashes, eager to redeem himself in his master's eyes and relieved to know that he'd soon be on his way.

Buckram chuckled to himself as he observed the young man's efforts. Silent workers: the best kind. He eased a loose half brick from the wall beneath the workbench and removed seventy pounds in notes of various denominations.

"Cato, I'm going away for a couple of days." Buckram's employee mimed concern and trustworthiness. "You are to officiate in my absence. Ensure the shop is locked at all times. Keep the place tidy. No assemblies. No friends, male or female. And no smoking. Understand?"

Cato led Juno out to the street. Buckram put on a pair of fur lined leather gloves while waiting for the stableboy to steady the stirrups for him. He mounted the horse in a smooth, unbroken motion.

"Here, Cato, a seasonal token for your good self." Buckram pressed a folded pound into the young man's hand. "And a merry Christmas to you!"

Cato's jaw dropped in amazement. He mouthed silent thanks as he stared at the money. And when he finally raised his eyes, Buckram was at the top of the road waving farewell.

Buckram let his horse canter down Long Acre and into Hog Lane. The ice was thick and smooth on the Tottenham Court Road where a deep chill muted even the smell from the brewery. He tied his scarf about his face while his steed trotted true. He enjoyed the feeling of being gloved and muffled on horseback. With just his eyes visible, he could have been anyone or nobody at all. A harsh wind buffeted them as they hit the open spaces along the Hampstead Road. He spurred Juno to a gallop and raced under the darkening skies, glad to be leaving London, if only to relish the taste of sweet, clean air.

He's charging through the white of winter, a black man on a black horse. He throws back his head and laughs in the cold, wild air. He is heading north now and speeding into Christmas Day, ready to claim whatever present the heart of England holds for him.